ADVENTURES IN
PIRATE COVE
THE HUNT FOR BURIED TREASURE

MARTYN GODFREY is an ex–junior high teacher who wrote his first book on a dare by one of his students. Since that time, he has written nearly thirty books for young people. Many of the humorous incidents in his stories originate from his fan mail. "I get lots of letters from young people," he explains. "Most of them tell me of a funny experience. It's great reading about the silly things that happen to people." Besides writing, Martyn's hobbies include growing older and collecting comic books.

2 ADVENTURES IN
PIRATE COVE
THE HUNT FOR BURIED TREASURE

MARTYN GODFREY

AN AVON CAMELOT BOOK

ADVENTURES IN PIRATE COVE #2: THE HUNT FOR BURIED TREASURE is an original publication of Avon Books. This work has never before appeared in book form.

AVON BOOKS
A division of
The Hearst Corporation
1350 Avenue of the Americas
New York, New York 10019

Copyright © 1996 by Martyn Godfrey
Published by arrangement with the author
Library of Congress Catalog Card Number: 95-96061
ISBN: 0-380-77502-6
RL: 5.2

First Avon Camelot Printing: June 1996

CAMELOT TRADEMARK REG. U.S. PAT. OFF. AND IN OTHER COUNTRIES, MARCA REGISTRADA, HECHO EN U.S.A.

Printed in the U.S.A.

OPM   10   9   8   7   6   5   4   3   2   1

To Mari and Chuck at the Saxony Motel,
Redington Beach, Florida:
Thanks for the work space.

A special thank-you to my son, Marcus,
for writing Andrew's letter.

chapter 1

I couldn't believe what I saw. Butcher Bortowski had his T-shirt yanked up and he was
digging around in his belly button. Deep. Real
deep. Past the second knuckle.

I glanced at Mr. Manning, our English teacher.
He was marking assignments, too focused to see
Butcher. I scanned the rest of the class. They
were writing or reading, unaware of Butcher's
strange behavior. I fought the urge to stand up
and shout, "Look at this, everyone! Look at what
Bortowski is doing!" Instead, I whispered to him.
"What are you doing, Butcher?"

"I'm checking it out," he whispered back.

I stared at Butcher's stomach, marveling at
how much tummy hair he had for an eighth
grader. "Checking out what?" I asked in my soft-
est voice.

Butcher pointed to his navel with his other
hand. "I thought I felt something moving around

in there," he murmured. "I don't want nothing living in my belly button again."

"Again? You had something alive in your belly button?"

He nodded. "Yeah, last spring."

"No kidding. What was it?"

"I don't know. By the time I got it out, it was all squashed up. It had a lot of legs and it was greeny-brown." He pulled his T-shirt down. "I'll check it good when I get home."

Mr. Manning looked up. "Is there a problem back there, boys?"

"No, sir," I answered.

Mr. Manning appeared as if he was going to question us further, but fortunately the last bell rang and he dismissed us.

As we gathered up our books, Butcher asked, "You still coming to my party tonight?"

"You bet. I'm still invited, huh?"

Butcher nodded. "Like I said on Monday, everybody's invited, even the nerds."

I laughed. "You're not talking about me when you say *even the nerds?*"

"You bet, I am."

"I'm not a nerd," I said.

"Yeah, you are. You got the word, Dweeb, tattooed on your forehead."

"Dweeb?"

"It's nothing personal, Hawgood. It's just a fact of life. Some guys are nerds. That's you. Some guys aren't. That's me. See you later." Butcher lumbered out of his desk and headed for the classroom door.

After wishing Mr. Manning a good weekend, I left the classroom and found my best friend, Delton Hayes, by his locker with a worried expression on his face. "What's up, Del? Did you see a black cat? Break a mirror? Lose your four leaf clover?"

Delton flashed me a get-off-my-case look. "I'm a little superstitious, so what?"

"A person who believes he's going to be in a plane crash if he puts his underwear on backwards is more than a little superstitious. And *you* believe that." I threw my books into my locker and grabbed my knapsack. "You want to come to my place and play Nintendo? My aunt sent my brother *Mortal Kombat 5* for his birthday."

"No, I can't. In sixth period computer class, I found a file on the Internet. A file for people who are a little superstitious, like me."

"Superstitious people talk to each other on the Internet?"

"All kinds of people talk about all kinds of things on the Internet. In the superstitious file, someone had left the message, 'If you carry a pinecone in September, you'll have good luck until December.' That's why I can't go to your house. I'm going to Lookoff Point to get a pinecone. There's a bunch of old white pines there. The message said, 'The older the tree, the more luck you'll see.'"

We closed our lockers at the same time and Delton went over to the drinking fountain, where he took a long drink.

"Do you think I'm a nerd," I said to the back of his head.

He straightened up and wiped his lips "Not really, why?"

"Not really? That doesn't sound like a *no*."

"Why do you think you're a nerd all of a sudden?"

"I don't. Butcher does."

Delton laughed. "Butcher thinks everybody in the whole world is a nerd, except him. And maybe Karlene Fraser."

"Karlene Fraser? The seventh grader? Butcher likes Karlene?"

"He's been eating lunch with her in the cafeteria all week. Haven't you noticed?"

"Butcher and Karlene, huh? Go figure. He's so big and she's so small. She looks like a second grader."

"You can't stop love," Delton observed. "She's the only seventh grader invited to his party tonight."

"Wow, Butcher Bortowski has a date. Life is strange," I noted. "Speaking of dates, are you nervous about Francine Buford tonight? You're going to meet her at Butcher's party. That's kind of like a date."

"It is?"

"It's enough of a date to mean you're going to spend a lot of time with her tonight. Does that make you nervous?"

"No, I *want* to hang out with Francine. Are you asking because of Stacey? You told Stacey you'd meet her at Butcher's too. Are you nervous about that?"

"Truth is, all week, I've been thinking maybe I'm going to do something stupid tonight and embarrass myself."

"Such as?"

"Like what if I'm dancing with Stacey and I belch in her face?"

Delton smiled. "I'd laugh at that." He waved good-bye and walked down the hall. "I'll see you at Butcher's."

When I got home I found my eight-year-old brother, Hornbeck, and his friend, Travis Bowman, making popcorn in the kitchen of Bed & Roses. Bed & Roses is the name of my grandmother's Bed and Breakfast House, the only B&B in Pirate Cove.

Hornbeck stood on a chair and peered into the clear plastic top of the hot air popcorn popper. Travis, his new best friend, sat in a chair with one of Gram's cats, Venus, on his lap, petting the old tabby.

I pitched my knapsack onto the counter. "Hi, guys."

"Hey, Garrett, you want to hear something my sister said?" Travis asked. "Something good she said about you? It'll only cost you ten bucks to find out."

Stacey said something about me, I thought. Good news! But I said, "I'm not going to pay you anything, Travis."

"Five bucks then."

"Nothing."

"Then I won't tell you."

"Yes, you will."

"You can't make me."

"Yes, I can. If you don't tell me, it'll be major underwear yank. Do you want the mother of all wedgies?"

"The mother of all wedgies?" Travis paled slightly. "You're bluffing. You wouldn't do that. I'll tell your grandmother."

"You'll be wearing your underwear around your ears when you do."

Travis thought about my warning. "Okay, be a bully. Pick on a poor, defenseless, little kid."

"What did Stacey say?" I insisted.

"I heard my sister tell my old man she's going to have a good time at Butcher's party. She told Dad she's going to have a good time 'cause you're going to be there. I think she's in love with you. All she does is talk about you. 'Garrett said this in Social Studies. Garrett did this in Science.' It makes me want to puke. I know you like her too. How can you like a girl?"

Travis asked the question as if liking a girl was the same as liking an overweight water buffalo.

"Some day Travis, girls will look different to you."

"Maybe," he said. "But I sure as heck ain't going to like a girl like Stacey. She's nuts."

Before I could defend Stacey, Hornbeck said, "The corn is swirling around inside, Garrett. But it's not popping yet. And the butter in the dish on top of the popper isn't melting either." My brother, his face still a few inches from the hot air popper, lifted the butter dish off the lid and leaned closer to check out the twirling kernels.

"Don't take the butter thing off," I warned. "That stops the corn from jumping out. I left it off once and the popcorn blew all over the floor. It was a real mess and . . ."

At that moment, a kernel reached its blow up point and exploded into Hornbeck's face. The little guy was so surprised, he jumped a foot off the chair. So surprised, he forgot what was in his hand. The butter dish flew into the air.

I know it happened in a second, two seconds at the most. It was certainly over before I could do anything to help. But it seemed to play out in slow motion. Hornbeck hovered in midair for what seemed the longest time. Then, very slowly, his feet returned to the chair. He landed lopsided, his socks skidding on the wooden seat. Off-balance, Hornbeck began a crazy dance of skittering feet and waving arms.

The chair lurched a little and Hornbeck's right foot slipped off the edge. My brother flew like a backward Superman, and landed with a loud thud on top of the kitchen table.

"Ow," he moaned.

The dish, on the other hand, became a miniature Space Shuttle, trekking up and up. The butter ended its flight with a wet *thadump* on the ceiling, where it cemented the dish to the stucco.

Venus tilted her head to survey the scene.

I glanced at Hornbeck. Then up at the stuck dish. Then at Travis.

"Wow," Travis said. "That was awesome. Do it again."

Hornbeck, on top of the table, had his eyes scrunched shut. "I hurt my bottom, Garrett."

I peered at the butter dish again and held my breath. In the same slow motion as Hornbeck's back flip from the chair, I watched the butter lose its grip; the dish peeled slowly off the ceiling. It sagged a quarter of an inch, twitched slightly, obeyed the law of gravity, and dropped loose.

And it turned upside down as it did.

My brother was directly in the line of descent.

I grimaced as a quarter pound of semisoft butter splattered across his face with a wet sloshing sound.

"Ow," Hornbeck shouted with feeling.

The plate slipped gently onto the table and spun like a tossed penny for a few seconds. It stopped beside Hornbeck's left ear.

"Cool," Travis exclaimed.

At that moment, the rest of the corn in the popper began exploding and the kitchen was instantly full of popped snow. Fluffy kernels rained down on the counter, the table, the chairs, on Hornbeck, on Travis, on Venus and me.

"All right!" Travis said.

I yanked the cord on the popper, rushed over and lifted the butter dish off Hornbeck. "Are you okay, Bro?"

Hornbeck sat up slowly, slid off the table and wiped at the yellow gunk on his nose. He didn't remove much, just smeared the butter around. "Yeah, I'm fine. Except for my rear end. I think you should have a look."

"No, thanks. Checking out your butt is not on my *To Do* list."

"Why are rotten things happening to me, Garrett?"

"You're definitely in accident mode, Hornbeck. But, don't worry, it's just a phase you're going through. I told you, I got into all kinds of accidents when I was in the third grade."

"I know," Hornbeck said. "You walked into a telephone pole and busted your nose."

"That's right." I touched my nose. "And it's still a little bent."

"Bent?" Travis noted. "You face goes one way and your nose goes the other."

"Watch it," I said.

Travis shrugged. "I'm just telling the truth."

"I guess you still want a wedgie to end all wedgies?" I warned.

"Okay, I take it back. Your nose is a *little* bent." Then I heard Travis whisper to himself. "And the Grand Canyon is a *little* hole."

I pretended I didn't hear. "Look on the bright side," I said to Hornbeck. "At least, you haven't broken any bones."

"Yet," he grumbled. "I haven't broken any bones yet." He rubbed his forehead, smearing more butter.

I handed him the dish towel. "You'd better go clean up."

"I'm jinxed." With slumped shoulders Hornbeck trudged out of the room.

I checked out the popcorn-covered kitchen and smiled. Despite the mess and Hornbeck's misfortune, it had been rather funny.

"Hey, Garrett," Travis said. "Tell me about sex. Tell me what they taught you in sixth grade Health class."

"Not a chance. You're going to have to wait three years."

"Fine, be a nerd. I don't care."

I remembered Butcher's comments. "You're just joking, right? You don't really think I'm a nerd, do you, Travis?"

"I'm not stupid enough to answer that," he said. "I don't want to walk around with turtleneck underwear." Travis looked down at Gram's cat, clamped his hands around Venus's front legs and lifted the old tabby into the air. "You know what, Garrett? I hear that if you drop a cat, it always lands on its feet. Is it okay if I go upstairs and throw Venus out the window?"

chapter 2

"**W**hat?" I said to Travis. "You want to drop Venus out of a window?"

"No, I want to throw her out."

"You want to throw Gram's cat out the window?"

"I'm just kidding, Garrett." Travis chuckled. "I'm not stupid. I don't want to throw no cat out no window. What do you think I am, a dorky little kid?"

I thought about it. "Yeah, I do."

Travis rubbed Venus behind her ears and the old cat purred. "My grandfather lives in Wisconsin," he said. "He has a farm with milk cows. He's got sixteen cats which live in his barn. I know all their names. There's Jaws, Claws, Pinky, Smoky, Fluffy. Then there's Traveler, Teddy, Sylvester, Sneeze, Rainbow and Dalmatian. The young ones are Splotches, Big Mama, Frisky, Wild Cat and Tracker. Cool names, huh?"

12

"Cool names," I replied. "Except for Sneeze. Your grandfather has a cat called Sneeze? Why would he name a cat Sneeze?"

He rolled his eyes. "Guess."

There was a polite knock on the door and Dr. McPherson, one of the guests at Bed & Roses, poked his head into the kitchen. "Can I come in, laddie?"

Dr. McPherson is a dentist from Scotland. He'd flown into Boston for a convention on Wednesday. On Thursday, he took the bus to Pirate Cove from the city and had to return for the rest of the convention on Saturday. He told Gram he was in Pirate Cove "on a family matter." Whatever that meant.

Of course, it made me curious, but I'd promised Gram I wouldn't be a pokey-pokey anymore. A pokey-pokey is how Gram refers to someone who won't mind his own business. And I admit to being more than a little nosy about some of our interesting guests.

A lot of colorful people stay with us in our B&B. By colorful, I mean different, unusual, eccentric or just plain weird. Our guests can be interesting because of how they behave, or walk, or eat, or whatever. Dr. McPherson is strange because everything about him is on the pudgy side. His stomach. His arms. His nose. His ears. Even his hair. The only hair he has left are two plump white tufts behind his temples.

13

Dr. McPherson appeared puzzled when he entered the kitchen and noticed the layer of popcorn.

I answered the unasked question. "My brother was making popcorn and we had a little accident."

"Auck, accidents happen," he replied in his broad Scottish accent.

I've always thought that was a stupid thing to say. *Accidents happen*. Of course, accidents happen. If accidents didn't happen, then there wouldn't be any accidents, would there?

I decided not to share my opinion with Dr. McPherson. "What can I do for you, sir?"

"I have a question about the wee laddie. Cornbuck, is it?"

"It's not Cornbuck," I corrected. "It's Hornbeck."

"I like that," Travis said. "Cornbuck. Neat. I got to go see how *Cornbuck* is doing." He grabbed a couple of pieces of popcorn off the counter, shoved them into his mouth and went in search of my brother.

"I saw Hornbeck in the hallway with butter on his face," Dr. McP said. "Is that some kind of game? Something the young people in America do?"

"No, we definitely don't butter our faces for fun. Let's just say it's something my brother does."

"Odd, but fascinating. If it's not too personal,

Garrett, I've been wondering about you two boys. Where are your folks then? Where's your mum and pop? How come you live with your gramma?"

"Our parents are weather scientists. They're away in Antarctica doing research on ozone holes for a couple of years. So Hornbeck and I are staying with Gram. We've been in Pirate Cove since last summer."

"I see then. Pirate Cove appears a jolly place. Staying here must be a very fine adventure."

"I guess, but sometimes I wish I was back in Vancouver. That's where we used to live. We're going to go back when my parents come home next year."

"There's no place like home," he said.

I figured that was another dumb thing to say. Of course, there's no place like home. Everybody's home is different.

"If you lived in a McDonald's, do you think you could say, 'There's thousands of places like home?'" I asked Dr. McPherson.

"I beg your pardon, boy."

"Nothing, sir. Look, I know you have to go back to Boston tomorrow, Dr. McP. But if you'd like to visit Hole's Island and the old mansion Saturday morning before the bus gets here, just let me know. I'll take you out on our boat. Do you know the story of Hole's Island?"

He hesitated for a moment, then said, "I have

heard a little. Maybe you could tell me some more."

I take guests staying at Bed & Roses out to Hole's Island to show them around. I've become an expert on the old place. I told Dr. McPherson everything I knew. "Just over a hundred years ago . . ." I began.

Hole's Island is a football field-long wedge of rock off the coast of Pirate Cove. The first thing you notice on Hole's Island is the century old mansion silhouetted against the sky. It was built by a rich New England sea captain, Frederick Hole, for his fiancée, a Scottish woman, Agnes McPherson. When Miss McPherson died before she came to America, the captain stopped building, and nobody ever got to live there.

On the other end of the island, hard to see from the shore, is the smaller ruin of a playhouse Hole was building for his future children. Of course, it was never used either.

I told Dr. McPherson about the island's history. Then I added, "It's sort of interesting that you and Captain Hole's fiancée have the same name, isn't it? Maybe you're related somehow."

Dr. McP pulled a white handkerchief from his pocket and dabbed the tiny beads of sweat on his bald head. "Now that's a thought."

"Captain Hole died in a shipwreck," I finished. "There's a story about how he left a treasure hidden somewhere on the island. We have a few treasure hunters visit Bed & Roses every year to explore the old buildings."

"And do you believe in the treasure, laddie?"

"I guess I do. Gram says there's so many rumors about it, there must be some truth somewhere in the past. I can take you out before you leave tomorrow. We can look for Hole's Treasure."

Dr. McP smiled. "Maybe we should do that. But I'm on a little search of my own. Something a little more personal than Captain Hole's Treasure."

"Oh, yeah? What?"

"I . . . I think I'd rather keep it to myself for now."

This was mysterious. What was he talking about?

"There's no need to look so bewildered, my boy. It's not a big secret. Just a little family quest, in a way. If I don't have any luck before I return to Boston, I'll let you in on it. Maybe you'll be able to find the timepiece."

"The timepiece? I don't have a clue what you're talking about, but you've got me awfully curious, sir," I told him.

He grinned, making a mass of dimples appear over his chubby face. "I'd better be on my way. Maybe I'll find good fortune before it gets dark."

Interesting, I thought. Most interesting.

*   *   *

17

My grandmother entered the kitchen after I cleaned up the popcorn.

"Garrett, would you vacuum and dust Second Floor Front, please? A couple from Vermont just faxed a reservation for Sunday."

I checked the stove clock. "Can I do it tomorrow? I want to play Nintendo for a bit. Then I have to shower and get ready for Butcher's party."

Gram made a sly smile.

"What?" I challenged. "How come you're looking at me like that?"

Her smile deepened. "Anxious to see that new girl, are we?"

"Stacey Bowman? Yeah, it'll be fun doing stuff with her."

"Stuff?" Gram wondered. "Do you mean you're hoping for a little kissy-face with Stacey?"

"I, what . . . *kissy-face?* What the heck is kissy-face?"

"That's what we called a little smooching in my day," Gram informed me.

"Kissy-face? Smooching? Give me a break, Gram."

"You can't fool me, Garrett Hawgood," she teased. "I see the look in your eyes. You're twitterpated."

"Twitterpated?" I buried my face in my hands. "Save me," I mumbled through my fingers. "My grandmother thinks she's a character from *Bambi*."

Gram actually giggled.

I tried to look stern. "I am not twitterpated. And I'm not hoping for a little kissy-face with Stacey."

"Whatever you say, Garrett. And you can clean Second Floor Front tomorrow. I'm always willing to help out when it comes to romance."

"I'm not—" I stopped. My grandmother could see right through me. So I changed the subject. "Gram, do you know what a nerd is?"

"Of course, I do. That's what I thought your father was when your mother brought him home for the first time. She came home from Harvard anxious for me to meet her new boyfriend, a Canadian from Vancouver. When he walked in the door I thought, 'What a nerd!' He was so skinny and those black frame glasses." She smiled. "But I'm so glad my daughter married him. If she didn't, I wouldn't have two wonderful grandsons spending a couple of years with me."

"If you saw me for the first time and you didn't know me, would you think I was a nerd too?" I asked.

"Why, that's a funny question."

"Think about it," I said.

She studied me for a long time and scratched her chin until it became red. Finally, she said, "It's such a silly question."

"Is that yes or no."

Gram checked the wall clock. "Didn't you say you had to get ready for a party?"

I could tell that, for whatever reason, Gram wasn't going to volunteer an opinion. So I pointed to the butter stain on the ceiling. "You might want to do something about that."

"Poop deck," Gram exclaimed. "How did butter get on our ceiling?"

"Cornbuck."

"Pardon me."

"You're going to have to ask Cornbuck."

"Cornbuck?" I heard her mumble as I left the kitchen. "What in heaven's name is a cornbuck?"

I went to the bedroom I share with Hornbeck, and played *Mortal Kombat 5* for ten minutes. Then I read a couple of pages in the latest Dennis Queen novel, *The Things*. I still had a hard time believing Dennis Queen was the pen name of the world's best horror writer, who was really Richard Bowman. And that Mr. Bowman was Butcher's uncle and the father of little Travis and the new girl in eighth grade, Stacey Bowman. And that he was going to buy a house and live with his family in Pirate Cove.

The truth is, I admire Dennis Queen because his horror stories are full of romance too. His heroes always know how to catch the girl. They always know the right things to say. I often wish I could be one of Dennis Queen's characters.

I thought about Dennis Queen's—Richard Bowman's—daughter.

I first saw Stacey when Mr. Nightingale, our assistant principal, walked into English class, interrupted Mr. Manning, and said, "Eighth graders, I'd like you to meet Stacey Bowman. She's starting in our school today. She's from away, but I'm sure you'll . . ." and so on.

I thought Stacey's long, straight hair, piercing green eyes, and lopsided smile redefined the meaning of cute. Add to that her Apache headband, poet blouse and floor-length flowered dress and I was looking at someone who made it hard to breathe. I knew I was hooked.

I sat on the edge of my bed and pictured Stacey Bowman and me inside an igloo in the middle of an Arctic blizzard.

"Oh, Garrett," Stacey says in my imagination. "I'm so frightened."

"There's no problem," I assure her. "The blizzard will be over in a week or two."

"Whatever are we going to do for all that time?" Stacey wonders.

"We'll think of something," I answer.

"It's so cold in here." Stacey shivers.

"Then I guess the first thing we should do is cuddle to stay warm. You know, hug and stuff."

Her face forms a frown. "Stuff? Do you mean like kissy-face?"

"Well, I suppose a little kissy-face wouldn't hurt if you were my girlfriend. Will you be my girlfriend?"

"Be your girlfriend?" she replies. "Why would I want to be your girlfriend?"

"Well," I stutter. "I'm a nice guy."

"You're an Aries," she says. "I'm a Scorpio. That's not a good match."

"We can work through it. Will you be my girlfriend?"

Stacey scratches her chin, deep in thought. It's such a cute chin. She scratches it some more. Scratches for a long time. Her chin is getting very red. At last, she answers. "I'll think about it."

Think about it?

This is my fantasy. Why does she have to think about it?

The phone rang, interrupting my thoughts of igloos. I picked it up. "Bed & Roses," I said.

"Garrett, come quick." It was Delton. But I'd never heard Delton sound like that. He was talking too loud and too high, breathing hard, either really scared or really excited. "Garrett," he panted. "You've got to help me."

chapter 3

"What's up, Del?" I said into the phone. "Are you all right?"

"I'm fine. I'm just going to need help. Come meet me. I've got to show you something. Right away."

"Okay, I'll be right there. You at home?"

"I'm calling from the pay phone on Little Dock. Get here as fast as you can."

The receiver clicked in my ear.

Little Dock, the northern boundary of Pirate Cove, is where the tourists tie their boats in the summer. It's the place where Shore Road ends. From there, Shore Road turns into The Stroll, a narrow walking path which hugs the shoreline for another two miles until it reaches Lookoff Point, a rugged rock cliff which overlooks the Atlantic. Tourists like The Stroll because it offers excellent views of the rocky shoreline on one side and thick forest on the other.

23

Little Dock juts from the only piece of Pirate Cove shoreline which has sand, instead of stones, covering the beach. No surprise it's called Sandy Beach. In August, Sandy Beach is full of people swimming, sunbathing, digging for clams and doing other beach things. After Labor Day, it's hardly used. Delton was alone, pacing back and forth on the boardwalk, nervously rubbing his frizzy hair.

As soon as I got close, he grabbed my arm and began to guide me from Shore Road to The Stroll like I was a little kid. "This way."

I tried to pull free. "What are you doing, Del?"

He let go. "Sorry. I guess I'm excited. I'll try to calm down. Follow me."

We traveled for a mile along The Stroll. All the time I kept prodding and pressing Del to tell me what was going on. "What have you found?" I asked a dozen times. Every time, he deflected my question, telling me it was something he couldn't explain. He would have to show me. As the minutes rolled on, I got more frustrated.

"I'm getting extremely frustrated by this," I told him.

After what seemed a decade later, Delton finally stopped. On our right, the water's edge was pebble beach. To our left, the land rose in a gentle slope through skinny trees. A massive boulder dominated the top of the small hill. Behind the large rock stood old-growth forest.

Delton pulled a small pinecone from his jeans pocket and waved it in front of my face. "I knew this would pay off. I wouldn't have found it, if it wasn't for my lucky pinecone."

"For the millionth time, found what? What are you talking about?"

"Okay, I walked to Lookoff Point, got this pinecone and was coming back when I got here and needed to pee. Now why would I need to pee right here?"

"Because of all the water you drank in school?"

"No, because my lucky pinecone made me think I had to go."

"Give me a break. That's totally dumb. For the millionth and oneth time, show me what you found."

Delton stepped left and threaded through the skinny trees up the slight hill toward the huge granite boulder. I traced his footprints.

"Just in case there was somebody on the trail, I walked up here. I didn't want anybody to see me." My friend slipped behind the boulder and I followed.

"And while I was going," Delton continued. "I thought I saw something behind the grass. Something carved in the rock." He pushed a clump of long grass aside with his shoe and pointed to an arm-length scar near the bottom of the boulder. "What's it look like, Garrett?"

There was no doubt what it was.

*   *   *

"It's an arrow," I told him."

"Course, it's an arrow. Why would somebody carve an arrow on this rock?"

"Maybe it wasn't carved. Maybe it's natural. Rocks get scratched up."

Delton shook his head. "It was chipped out. A long time ago."

"How do you know that?" I wondered.

"Rub your finger along the arrow."

I did.

"What do you feel?" he asked.

"Bumps," I answered.

"That means the arrow was chipped out, bit by bit. Do you notice how the bumps aren't sharp? If you chip rock, the edges are sharp. After a lot of years, rain and snow and wind wear the rock away. Sharp bumps become smooth bumps."

"You sound like a Science teacher."

"If someone carved it here, then it must be pointing to something."

My eyes followed the direction of the arrow into the forest. "There's nothing that way. Just trees. Trees all the way to the next town, Bay of Bays."

Delton nodded. "Right. Lots and lots of trees. Now let's pretend you found a special tree. What would you do if you wanted to find that same special tree again in ten years?"

"Why would I want to find a tree ten years from now?"

"Play along, Garrett. What would you do?"

"I guess I'd mark the tree, so I'd know which one it is."

"That's a good idea, Garrett. But there's a big problemo with it. In ten years, the forest will change. New trees and bushes will grow. Your tree could look different. You could be wandering around for hours, maybe days, looking for your special mark. What if you wanted to find your tree real fast?"

I understood what he was getting at. "I'd mark something that wouldn't change. Something like a boulder."

He patted my shoulder. "You got it. Follow me."

Once again, I trailed my buddy through the pines, oaks and maples.

"I tried to stay in a straight line from the boulder," Delton said.

I followed in silence, occasionally glancing up at the canopy of leaves blowing gently in the ocean breeze. The sun thrust through, making leaf shadows dance and spin on the forest floor. The salty Atlantic air mixed with the leafy-sweet humidity of the forest. Birds chirped and squawked. Pinecones occasionally scrunched under our shoes. In some places the saplings were really thick and we had to squeeze and duck between bark and branches. We plodded on for ten minutes.

"When I got here, I was about to give up," Delton declared. "At this point, I was starting to think my theory could be wrong. But I went a little further." He waved me onward.

Fifty yards deeper into the woods we came to a small clearing dominated by one of the largest oak trees I'd ever seen. Its massive branches were thicker than the trunks of most of the other trees. It would take six people, holding hands, to make a circle around it.

"This is a special tree somebody, a long time ago, wanted to find again," Delton said. "It's got to be two hundred years old. Maybe older."

"If you say so, Del." I paced a complete circle around the oak's trunk, looking for a mark, dent, or anything different. All I saw was rough bark. "How do you know this has anything to do with the arrow on the rock? I don't see anything."

"That's because you're looking in the wrong spot. Look down."

Again, I did as I was told. I saw grass growing in sandy soil. Some plants I didn't know the names of. A circle of toadstools. A feather. Nothing else. "What am I looking for?"

"Where we're standing is lower than the rest of the ground," Delton pointed out.

He was right. We stood in an almost perfect square, six feet by six feet, half a foot lower than the rest of the forest floor.

"This isn't normal," I said. A couple of very

weird thoughts flashed through my head. Like this was where a UFO landed. Maybe it was a secret missile silo. Dumb stuff I knew couldn't be true. "What do you think it is, Del?"

"You ever hear about The Money Pit on Oak Island?" Delton asked.

I shook my head.

"I did a book report on it in sixth grade. It's an island off of Nova Scotia. There's a big pit on the island which is supposed to be full of treasure which nobody has found yet. The guys who discovered it noticed something just like this. A square, low spot in the ground. It was made when the dug-up dirt settled. I think somebody dug a hole here. Over the years, the dug-up dirt packed tighter. That's why it's over a half foot lower."

The excitement gave my guts a squeeze. "You could be right, Del."

"I'm pretty sure I am. What else could it be? Like you said, it isn't normal."

"Interesting."

"Very interesting. Next question. Why would somebody dig a hole in this spot?"

I shrugged.

"People dig holes because they want to bury something," Delton said. "Look around. Can you think of any reason why somebody would want to bury something right here?"

"No," I answered.

"Of course not. It's deep in the woods. It's hard

29

to find. It takes a half hour to get here from town. There's absolutely no reason to bury anything here. Unless . . ." He paused. "Unless you wanted to bury something you wanted to keep a secret. Something you didn't want other people to find. Do you know who I think dug a pit here?"

A thought crossed my mind, but I didn't want to say it out loud. It was just too incredible.

"Captain Frederick Hole," Delton answered his own question. "This might be Captain Hole's treasure pit, Garrett. I mean, it makes sense when you think about it. Captain Hole came here, buried his treasure, then spread the rumor he'd hidden it somewhere on the island. Nobody would bother to look for his loot on the mainland if they thought it was on Hole's Island, would they? It's a perfect plan. He was going to come back and get it later. But he drowned without telling anyone his secret."

I thought about it. "That's a real stretch, Del."

"You don't believe me?"

"Let's just say the logic is hard to believe."

"Why?" he asked.

"For one thing, how come nobody found it before now?"

"Because even if somebody did come here, they wouldn't know what they were looking at, would they? It looks like any other part of the woods. And the arrow on the rock can't be seen from The Stroll."

"I don't know," I hedged.

Del's grin showed a mouthful of teeth. "If this is Captain Hole's pit, I guess it means I'm rich. A treasure from a hundred years ago must be worth a hundred times more today. It's like winning the lottery. I'll be able to ride to school in a limo. Go to Boston to see the Sox or the Bruins whenever I want. Eat lobster every day. And, if this is Hole's Treasure, like I think, then because you're my best friend, I'll give you part of it for helping me dig."

"Um, thanks, Del," I muttered. "That's really generous of you."

"I know," he said. "Besides, there's a saying, 'If you don't share, you lose your hair,' so I have to share with somebody. I mean I don't want to be bald."

"Listen, Del, maybe you shouldn't get your hopes up. Even though it makes sense, I find it kind of hard to believe you found Hole's Treasure when other people have been looking for it for over a century."

"That's because they were looking in the wrong place." Delton raised his fists and punched the air. "I found Hole's Treasure." He took two steps forward and hugged me for a few seconds.

I stiffened. "Er, what are you doing, Del?"

When he realized he had his arms around me, he pulled away. "You're going to have to keep it a secret, Garrett. If we tell anyone, then they could tell somebody else and soon the whole town will know. Your grandmother will understand. My folks will understand. When I come home with my pockets full of gold and jewels, they'll understand."

"Okay. But Gram always says, 'Don't count your chickens before they hatch.' "

"What has this got to do with birds?" he wondered.

"It means you shouldn't count on there being gold and jewels under here."

"Let's get some shovels, then," he suggested. "We might be able to find what's buried here before dark."

I think if I was convinced my buddy had found Hole's Treasure, I would have jumped to the chore immediately. But I was far from persuaded. Far, far from swayed.

I remembered watching a *National Geographic* special about treasure hunting on PBS. You didn't find treasure by dumb luck. It was hard work. The guy who found the *Titanic* searched for it for years. And he knew where it was.

I was excited because there was a slim chance this *was* Captain Hole's long-ago stashed loot. But the odds against it meant I had another priority.

"Let's dig tomorrow morning," I said. "It's Butcher's party tonight."

"So what? Digging up Hole's Treasure is more important than a party."

"It's not just any party. I want to see Stacey. And you promised Francine you'd meet her there." I tapped the ground with my right sneaker. "What's under here isn't going to go anywhere, is it? It'll wait until tomorrow."

"If you say so," Delton didn't sound convinced.

"If you're right and it is Hole's Treasure," I reasoned. "It's been there for over a hundred years. And it'll be here twelve hours from now. Think about Francine. You said you were looking forward to spending time with her."

So he thought about it. "Okay, for Francine then," he said reluctantly. "But tomorrow morning, we come back and dig. We come back early."

"We come back early," I agreed.

chapter 4

I sat in the family room of Butcher Bortowski's house and checked out the other people at the party. Fifteen of us, including Butcher, Wendy, Stephen, Patricia, Donnie, Abdul and Delton's kind-of-date, Francine Buford. And, as Del said, Karlene Fraser, the seventh grader.

Francine saw me looking at everyone and flashed a miffed expression in my direction. I guessed she was upset because Delton hadn't arrived yet. Where was he anyway? After we left the clearing and walked back to Pirate Cove, he told me he was going to go home, change, and come straight to Butcher's.

I smiled at Francine, then checked out Butcher for a few moments. He was sitting on the couch with Karlene. The big guy wore a smug look as he patted his belly over the top of his heavy-metal muscle shirt. I wondered if that meant he'd found whatever was inside his belly button.

34

Karlene was scrunched beside him, as close as she could get, with her arms wrapped around his massive right bicep. They were such a strange couple; he was so huge and she was so tiny. King Kong dates Thumbelina, I thought.

I quickly lost interest in Butcher and Karlene when Stacey Bowman entered the room. As I said, Stacey is Butcher's cousin. She and her family are staying with the Bortowski's until they buy their own house in Pirate Cove.

Stacey was dressed in a tie-dyed, neon blue T-shirt and tight, faded, frayed bell-bottom blue jeans. I figured a girl couldn't get any better-looking.

Stacey waved to me and mouthed, "Hello, Garrett."

It was such a natural wave, a gentle gesture of her hand. "No girl anywhere in the world can wave as cute as that," I said to myself.

I stood up with the plan of marching straight toward Stacey, but Francine stood up at the same time and blocked my path.

"Do you have any idea where Delton is?" Francine asked. "He said he was going to be here by seven. That's a half hour ago."

"We were a little late because Del and I were doing something," I explained. "But you're right; he should be here by now. He has a superstition about being late. He thinks he'll get pimples if he's not on time."

35

"I'm a little worried," Francine said.

Maybe I should check it out, I thought. Considering what Delton may have found and all. Delton wouldn't have changed his mind and gone back to dig alone, would he?

"I'll go phone him, Francine."

I went into the Bortowski's kitchen. Mr. Bortowski stood by the stove, making a humongous pot of instant mashed potatoes. Mr. Bortowski is Butcher in thirty years, bigger, tougher and hairier. My mother and Mr. B. were friends when they were kids. Mom says they even dated for a while in high school, although I have no idea what they had in common.

"Is it okay if I use the phone, Mr. B.?"

Mr. Bortowski stirred the food with a fork, nodded in the direction of the wall phone, and began to attack the potful of potatoes. By the time I called Delton's house, let it ring ten times without an answer, and hung up, Butcher's dad had scarfed the food and scraped the pot clean. He burped loudly and wiped his lips on the sleeve of his T-shirt. "That's better. I was a little hungry. Working on the ElectraGlide is hard work."

Butcher told everyone his Dad's Harley-Davidson motorbike had been sitting in the garage for over ten years. Butcher bragged how he was helping his father get the bike running again. The big guy said it was going to be his bike when he turned sixteen.

36

"How is the Harley?" I wondered.

"I almost got her purring like an angry tom-cat," Mr. B. declared. "Maybe tomorrow I'll take her for a run. I've had that bike nearly thirty years. I used to take your mom for rides on it back in high school."

"I hope I get to own a Harley one day," I said.

"Hey," Mr. Bortowski replied. "Everybody hopes they own a Harley one day. Enjoy the party, Garrett."

Butcher's dad left the kitchen and I was about to do the same when Stacey entered. "I wondered where you went, Garrett." She flipped her head which made her long hair swirl across her shoulders, another natural, cute move, and opened the fridge. It was stuffed with cans of soda. She shuffled them aside to get a bottle of Perrier. "I don't drink anything but natural source mineral water." She twisted off the bottle top and took a little sip. "What's your most personal possession? You can tell so much about a person when you discover what they treasure the most. What do you own that you'd hate to lose. Other than your family and friends."

"I've never thought about it."

"Think about it now," she encouraged. "Is it a favorite toy? Or maybe a teddy bear from when you were little? You do still have your teddy bear, don't you?"

I felt suddenly embarrassed. Dare I tell Stacey

my teddy bear sits on the shelf above my bed? I decided not to mention it.

"Well, I guess the thing I like the most is my 1961 Roger Maris baseball card. That's the year after Maris broke Babe Ruth's home run record. My grandfather left it to me in his will. It's worth a lot of money now."

"So you treasure it because it's worth money?"

"No, because there aren't that many of them around."

My answer seemed to please her. "That's why I treasure my most valuable possession too. It's a mote from the moon."

"A mote? What's that?"

"A tiny piece of dust. My father wrote a book about an alien who takes over Cape Kennedy."

"I know. I read it."

"The people at NASA liked it so much, they gave my father a tiny piece of moon dust *Apollo 14* brought back to Earth. Dad gave it to me for my twelfth birthday. It's still packed in a moving box, but I'll show it to you someday. It's inside a solid piece of plastic."

"That would be neat."

"Do you believe in reincarnation, Garrett?"

"Reincarnation? Like dying and coming back as somebody else?"

She nodded. "I've been reading all about it. Some people believe your soul goes through many lives. All week, I've been trying to regress. That means I've been trying to remember my former lives. Every night, just before I fall asleep, I try to let the memories of my past lives rise to the surface."

What a weird thing to do. But, coming from Stacey, I liked the idea. I'd never met anyone like her before. I found her weirdness really attractive.

"I think I know who I was in my last life," Stacey went on. "I was a hippie. My name was Herman. I went to Woodstock. I passed on when I fell off a cliff."

Herman The Hippie? Fell off a cliff? Something was familiar. It seemed like someone had told me something like that. Where had I heard that story before?

I locked my fingers together, twiddled my thumbs nervously, then promptly stopped when I realized how nerdy I must have looked. I took a deep breath. "Would you like to dance with me later, Stacey?"

She smiled. "I'd like that, Garrett. Even though I've only known you for a few days I know you're a kindred soul."

"Kindred?"

"It means you and I are close somehow. Maybe we knew each other in a previous life." She leaned toward me and planted a kiss on my cheek. "I've decided I like you," she whispered into my ear.

Then I noticed we weren't alone in the kitchen. Butcher had joined us. He was standing by the doorway into the family room, arms folded across his chest, an angry look on his face.

"I don't like what I just saw, Stacey," he growled. "Kissing Garrett is not a good move. I warned you about him."

"Warned her about me?" I asked. "What do you mean by that, Butcher?"

"You think school is fun. You can't trust anybody who thinks school is fun. They grow up to be teachers and I hate teachers."

"You ever stop and listen to yourself?" I asked. "You ever notice how stupid you sound?"

Butcher tightened his fists and waved them in the air. "You looking for a little talk with these?"

"Get bent, Butcher," I shot back. "You don't scare me." Which, of course, was a light-year away from the truth.

"Guys," Stacey said. "It's a party. Let's not spoil it."

Butcher grumbled something under his breath, scratched his gut, then nodded. "Right. Why should I let a nerd spoil my party? I'd like you two to come back to the family room. I got a surprise."

Stacey trailed her cousin into the family room, and I followed her.

"Now that we've got everyone, I got a surprise. We're going to start with a couple of games,"

Butcher announced. "Games are a good way to make a party roll. The first game we're going to play is Sandwich Crunch."

"Sandwich Crunch?" Francine asked. "I've never heard of it. How do you play it?"

"Easy," Butcher said. "Two people play the bread and they run around trying to sandwich people between them. It's a hoot. Sometimes you get to crunch somebody so hard, they can't breathe."

Karlene let out a squeaky giggle. "Oh, how exciting."

"Butcher," Stacey said. "I'm not going to partake in any activity so violent. Games should develop harmony between people."

"Huh?" Butcher regarded Stacey as if he didn't have a clue what she was talking about. Which, of course, he didn't. So he tried a second suggestion. "Okay, how about we play Jam Tag? We get a spoon and a jar of jam and the person who is *it* tries to peg you with a spoonful of jam. You get two points if you hit someone in the head, five points for the face and ten points if you cream their butt. My brother, Baker, and me play it all the time. The good part about it is you get to suck your clothes clean when you finish."

"Oh, how exciting." Karlene repeated her squeaky giggle.

"I think I speak for everyone when I say none of us wants to suck our clothes clean," I said. "We just want to talk and, maybe, dance. Do you think you could put on some music?"

"We dance later," Butcher said. "First we play some kind of game. How about Spin the Bottle? It ain't the little kid kissing game. We spin a bottle and if it points to you, you have to tell the most embarrassing thing that's ever happened to you." He grabbed a half-empty two-liter bottle of Coke from the coffee table, swallowed the contents in one gulp, belched, and sat on the floor. "Sit down."

Apparently, nobody objected to playing Butcher's version of Spin the Bottle because they quickly sat on the rug, forming an egg-shaped circle. Karlene sat next to our host and, once again, clamped her arms around his bicep. I joined the circle halfheartedly.

I checked the clock above the fireplace. It was way past seven-thirty.

Now, I was more than a little worried about Delton. It was so unusual for him to be late.

Butcher's little brother, Baker, who is in the same class as Hornbeck and Travis, came into the room. "Hey, Butcher, can I play?"

"No way," Butcher shot back. "Get lost."

Baker gave his brother a small shove.

"Stupid, little creep," Butcher grumbled.

"How can you say that, Butcher?" Francine wanted to know. "He's just a cute, little kid."

"Yeah? Well, that cute, little kid peanut buttered my underwear last night," Butcher replied.

"Peanut buttered your underwear?" Francine asked.

"You don't want to know," I told her.

Butcher placed the bottle on the carpet with his right hand. "I'm going to spin it. If it stops with the top pointing at you, then you have to tell your most embarrassing moment. And no keeping back. You got to tell the truth."

chapter 5

Butcher grinned, pleased to be playing his own version of Spin the Bottle, and gave the empty soda bottle a spin. It revolved madly for a few seconds, then stopped, pointing at Stacey.

Before Stacey could say anything, Butcher laughed. "This one is easy," he said. "I already know her most embarrassing moment. Baker walked into the bathroom last night and saw Stacey perched on the pot." He laughed again. "Do you guys know she has a big mole on her—"

"Butcher!" Stacey snapped. "Don't say another word."

I thought about Baker's experience. Wherever the mole is, it must be a cute mole, I reasoned.

"I've had people walk in on me when I've been going to the bathroom a couple of times too," Francine said. "It's embarrassing, but it's certainly not the most embarrassing thing that can

44

happen. It's not like you're the only person in the world who has to go to the bathroom, is it? Do you have something more embarrassing than that, Stacey?"

Stacey's scowl turned into a smile for Francine. "As a matter of fact, I do. Last year I went to a Psychic Fair in Orlando, where I used to live."

"A psycho fair?" Butcher asked. "Is that a place for crazy people to go and hang out?"

"Oh, how exciting," Karlene squeak-laughed.

Stacey sighed, deep and long. "It's a big convention where fortune tellers from all over North America get together and you can pay them to read your future."

"Oh, that stuff," Butcher said. "That junk is all crapola."

"Go on, Stacey," somebody said.

"Madam Gunther was there," Stacey continued. "Madam Gunther is a world famous—"

"Loser," Butcher interjected. "Madam Gunther is a world famous geek."

"Butcher!" several of us snapped.

This time Stacey ignored her cousin. "She's a world famous crystal ball reader. People say her predictions are right almost all of the time. So I stood in line for over two hours to have Madam Gunther read my fortune. I don't know if it was because it was so hot, or so crowded or something I ate. But when I finally got to the front of the line, I threw up on her crystal ball."

"Excellent!" Butcher said. "Sprayed chunks all over. Decent. Guess Madam Geek learned how to tell the future in your used cookies, huh?"

Butcher grabbed the bottle and spun it a second time.

The bottle slowed and landed on Donnie.

"My most embarrassing moment?" Donnie thought out loud. "I guess it was when I was in the first grade. Some big kids . . ." He laughed to himself. "Big kids? Maybe they were fifth graders. Whatever, they caught me in the bathroom, grabbed my arms and head, and gave me a swirly. The ultimate insult. They put me on my knees, shoved my head into the toilet and flushed."

"Yuck," Francine said.

"Lucky there was nothing in the toilet at the time," Donnie finished. "Other than my head."

"That's a good one, Donnie," Butcher said as he spun the bottle for the third time.

It stopped on Butcher.

"I got nothing to say," he told us. "I got nothing to say because I never get embarrassed."

"I don't think that's true," Francine said. "I remember back in the first grade and the class walked over to the high school to watch a football game against Bay of Bays. You climbed under the bleachers and hid under the first row of seats. You lay down on the ground so you could look up the cheerleaders' skirts. When the teacher found you, she couldn't stop laughing. You were so embarrassed you started crying."

"I wasn't crying. I had something in my eye. I wasn't embarrassed."

"Bull feathers," Francine said.

"I don't want to talk about it." Butcher spun the Coke bottle yet again. This time it landed on me. And I was glad it did. I figured I could get Stacey to like me even more by telling a most embarrassing moment.

"Knowing you, Garrett," Butcher said, "your most embarrassing moment is going to be dopey."

"Butcher, stop being such a dork," Stacey said. "You're spoiling the ambience of the party."

"What?" he said. "I ain't trying to wreck the ambulance of nothing."

"Ambience," Francine corrected. "It means the mood. And Stacey is right. Maybe you could let Garrett tell his story without adding your two cents worth?"

"Maybe I could do that," Butcher said. "But I don't think I will 'cause I don't want to. Tell your dopey story, Garrett."

Back in sixth grade, one of my electives was Public Speaking. Mrs. Pratt, our teacher, showed us how to play upon the emotions of an audience. I hoped I remembered everything she'd taught me.

"My most embarrassing moment happened when I was in kindergarten," I began. "We were watching a nature show. A mother deer and her fawn were being chased by a pack of wolves. The deer jumped into the river and swam. Luckily, the wolves didn't follow. The mother had no trouble climbing up the bank on the other side. But . . ." I paused just like Mrs. Pratt taught me.

Stacey's eyes were riveted on me. Everyone was waiting to hear what happened next. Even Butcher seemed slightly interested.

"But what?" Francine prodded.

"But the little baby deer couldn't get up the steep bank. He'd struggle up, lose his footing, and fall back into the water," I said in a sympathetic voice. "I was so worried for the little guy."

I noted the concern in Stacey's eyes. She was really into my story.

I spoke real slow to get a dramatic effect. "That little deer tried for what seemed like hours to get onto the land." I paused again, milking their interest in how the story was going to end. "Once, it slipped and vanished under the river. I was sure it drowned. But . . . but then, its skinny front legs flopped onto the bank and the back legs skittered out of the water. It made it. The little baby shook the water off and rubbed noses with its mother."

"Then the deer fell back in, drowned, and was washed up rotten and smelly in the spring," Butcher said.

"Oh, how exciting," Karlene laughed in her mouse-like squeak.

"That was great, Garrett," Francine said. "You really know how to tell a story."

Thanks to Mrs. Pratt, I thought.

"It was a good story," Donnie agreed. "But did I miss something? What's embarrassing about it?"

"The embarrassing part came next," I said. "As the deer climbed the riverbank, you could see the love between them."

"What?" Butcher grunted. "You could *see the love?* Between deer? That sounds like sissy talk. You sure you're a normal guy, Hawgood?"

"Garrett is sensitive," Stacey said to Butcher.

"Anyway," I finished. "I crawled over and hugged the TV. I wanted those deer to know how I felt. But you know what five year olds are like? Everybody in the class started calling me TV Hugger. In the playground, they'd come up to me and sing, 'T-V Hug-ger. T-V Hug-ger.' That was the embarrassing part."

"Dumb," Butcher said. "A sissy story."

Mr. Bortowski entered the room chomping on two slices of pizza, one upside-down on the other. "Hey, Garrett," he said through a mouthful of cheese and pepperoni. "I've got a message for you."

Darn, I thought, just when I was going to milk the story, make Stacey see what a soft-hearted guy I was. "What's the message, Mr. B.?"

"Delton just called and said to meet him at the rock right now. He said to get there as fast as you can."

The rock? That had to be the rock with the arrow on it.

"Is everything okay?" Francine wanted to know.

"Yeah, what's up?" Butcher asked suspiciously. "Are you and Hayes up to something?"

"I have to go," I announced.

"What are you guys up to?" Butcher demanded.

It has to be something about Delton's discovery, I thought.

What could be wrong?

chapter 6

I quickly said my good-byes and left the Bortowski house. I was halfway down their front path when I heard, "Garrett, wait a minute."

I stopped and turned as Stacey joined me. "Is everything all right with Delton?"

"I can't think of anything that could be wrong."

Which was true. What could be wrong about the rock or sunken ground? Yet at the same time, I knew something *was* wrong. Delton would be at the party if everything was okay. He wouldn't have phoned if everything was all right.

"I just wanted you to know how moving your embarrassing moment with the deer was," Stacey said. "That was such a sensitive thing to do. I've never met a boy as sensitive as you. I'm sure you and I must have known each other in a former life."

As long as we're close in this life, I thought. "Maybe I was one of Herman The Hippie's friends."

"If you were, you were a very close friend. Maybe you were Herman's girlfriend," she suggested.

"Now that's definitely a weird thought," I said.

She took my hand and squeezed it. "I hope you can come back to the party, Garrett. Au revoir."

I watched her walk back into the Bortowski home. Even her walk is cute, I thought. The way she sort of bounces with each step is so attractive.

And then a wave of guilt showered over me.

My folks and Gram have strong ideas of what's right and wrong. And they've passed on their ideas to Hornbeck and me. One of the things they'd taught me is, it's wrong to lie. Lies only get you into trouble.

"You tell a lie," Mom once said. "And pretty soon you have to tell another lie to cover up the first lie and another lie to cover up the second and soon things get out of hand. And when someone discovers you've lied, that person will never, ever trust you again."

And I'd lied to Stacey.

Heck, I'd lied to half the kids in my eighth grade class. I'd lied and I hadn't thought anything about it at the time. I did it to get what I wanted. And what I wanted was to have Stacey like me more.

The embarrassing story about hugging the TV after the deer escaped the pack of wolves was a true story. The problem was, it wasn't my story. It had happened to my brother. Hornbeck was the poor little guy who had to put up with the teasing about being a TV Hugger. Not me. Every time Mom told somebody about Hornbeck's TV hugging, they thought it was an *adorable* tale. That's why I told it as if I'd done it. I figured Stacey would think the same thing.

And she did.

After all, she had come outside to tell me how sensitive I was. That was wonderful. That's what I wanted.

So why did I feel so guilty about it then?

Why did it make me feel bad when it should be making me feel great?

When I reached the end of Shore Road, I tried to push the feeling to the back of my mind and broke into a jog. While running down The Stroll, I picked up the igloo-in-a-raging-blizzard fantasy in my imagination.

"You'll think about it?" I wonder. "Why do you have to think about being my girlfriend, Stacey? This is my fantasy. How come you didn't say yes?"

Stacey nibbles on a piece of frozen cheese and studies the flame on the blubber lamp. "I can't answer that question, can I? Like you said, it's your fantasy. You'll have to figure it out."

So I try. "Maybe it was because, in real life, I didn't know if you liked me. That could be why you said, 'I'll think about it' in my daydream. Now I know you like me in real life, maybe you'll say yes if I ask you again."

"Maybe."

"Will you be my girlfriend, Stacey?"

"Yes."

"That's great."

"Would you like to kissy-face now, Garrett?"

"Sure."

She closes her eyes, puckers her lips and leans toward me. I lean toward her.

"Wait!" she shouts, opening her eyes. "Wait a minute. Before we kissy-face, I have to know if you're sensitive. I could never kiss a boy who wasn't sensitive."

"Well, of course I am. You can ask anybody."

"Prove it, Garrett. Prove you're sensitive."

"Okay, when I was in kindergarten I saw a TV show where a couple of deer escaped from a pack of wolves. I went over and hugged the TV."

"Most astral. You really are sensitive."

She closes her eyes again, puckers her lips and leans toward me. I lean toward her.

"Wait!" she shouts, opening her eyes. "Wait a minute. I've heard that story before. Your mother told it to me."

"My mother? My mother is in Antarctica. How did you speak to my mother?"

"Stop asking me questions I can't answer. I told you, this is your fantasy."

"Things are not going the way I want them to," I mumble.

"Well, they're going to get worse, Garrett," Stacey threatens. "Because when your mother told me about the deer and the wolves and the TV hugging, she said your little brother, Hornbeck, was the one who did it."

"My mother told you that?"

Stacey nods.

"What if I told you my mother wasn't telling the truth?"

Stacey shakes her head. "I wouldn't believe you. Mothers never ever lie."

"Sure they do," I point out. "They tell you needles won't hurt. Vegetables taste good. Santa Claus is a jolly elf. The tooth fairy likes giving money away. You ever wonder what the tooth fairy does with all those teeth? I mean, what do you do with billions and billions of teeth?"

"Don't try to change the subject," she scolds. "Moms always tell the truth. If she said Hornbeck hugged the TV, then Hornbeck hugged the TV. You didn't."

"Are you saying I'm a liar?" I ask.

"Yes."

"Does that change your mind? Do you still want to be my girlfriend?"

"No. Not anymore."

Poof!

55

*   *   *

The imaginary igloo vanished from my thoughts. I shouldn't have lied, I thought.

Fortunately, I didn't have to dwell on it any longer because I reached my destination. I discovered an impatient and nervous Delton waiting on The Stroll by the arrow rock.

"There you are," he said in his hyper voice. "I was wondering if you got the message. When I hung up the phone, I knew I should have talked to you myself. I wanted to call you back, but I didn't have another quarter. You know how the Bortowskis are. You can't really trust them when it comes to giving messages and things like—"

"Hey," I interrupted. "Slow down. You're talking a mile a minute."

"Okay. Okay." He took a deep breath and blew it out slowly. "We've got big trouble, Garrett. We've got a big, big problem."

"What?"

"Your guest, the Scottish guy . . ."

"Dr. McPherson?"

"Yeah, him. He's searching for Hole's Treasure."

"How do you know that?"

"Well, when I left my house to go to Butcher's, I saw McPherson walking down by Little Dock, which I thought was a little weird because there's nothing there after the summer is over. Then I thought, so what's the big deal? He's on vacation.

56

He's going on a walk. I mean, tourists pay big bucks to be near the ocean, don't they? But then, McPherson vanished into The Stroll. So I followed him."

"Why? He could have been going to Lookoff Point."

"I had a feeling. You know, one of those feelings where you just *know* something bad is going down. Anyway, it didn't take me long to catch up to him because he was walking real slow and checking into the trees. I think he was looking for the rock."

"Why do you think that?"

"Because when he saw the boulder, he stopped and looked at it for the longest time. Then he took some papers out of his pocket and read them. Then he marched up and started checking the rock."

"Did he see the arrow?"

"How could he miss it?"

"What did he do?"

"He walked into the woods and I couldn't see him anymore."

"Why didn't you follow him?"

"There was no way I'd do that. I mean, what if I followed McPherson and the guy tried to kill me because I know where the treasure is buried? So I ran to the pay phone on Little Dock."

I squinted. "So you called me so he can kill both of us?"

Delton nodded. "There's safety in numbers."

"Thanks a lot, buddy."

"What are we going to do, Garrett?"

I looked into the sky. It was getting dark fast. "We're going to go back to Bed & Roses," I told him. "It's almost night. In a half hour, you won't be able to see your hand in front of your face, let alone a couple of thousand trees."

"So we go back and get flashlights?" Delton asked.

"No way. It's going to get dark for Dr. McPherson too. He'll have to return to Bed & Roses soon. Let's wait for him there."

I thought about the strange conversation Dr. McP and I had in the kitchen. What was it our guest had said? Something about his family. "I'm on a little search of my own. Something a little more personal than Captain Hole's Treasure." That was it.

Delton jumped. "Hey," he whispered. "Did you see that?"

"See what?"

My friend pointed back down The Stroll. "I thought I saw somebody behind those bushes over there."

I squinted, trying to make out details in the rapidly increasing gloom. "There's nobody there."

"It sure looked like a face. You weren't followed, were you?"

"Course not. Why would anybody follow me?"

Delton exhaled, long and deep and loud. "I guess I'm just seeing things."

"I'm uptight too, Del. But I think everything will be okay. I have a feeling you're wrong. Dr. McP may not be looking for Hole's Treasure. He may be looking for something else."

My friend reached over and patted a tree. "Touch wood everything is still okay. Touch wood Hole's Treasure is still mine."

Delton and I beat Dr. McPherson home by twenty minutes. When he walked through the door of Bed & Roses, we looked like we were casually playing a game of Crazy Eights in the sitting room. Actually, we'd been practicing what we were going to ask him. I'd told Delton to let me do the talking.

"Hi, Dr. McPherson," I said as he closed the front door. "Can I talk to you a minute?"

An archway separates our sitting room from the hall. Dr. McP stepped into the archway and rested his bulk on the wall.

"How's it going, sir?" I asked.

"Going, laddie? Just fine." He patted his bald head with his handkerchief. "Hot today. Very hot. Went for a long walk."

"Where did you walk to, sir?"

"Along The Stroll," he answered. "Pirate Cove is such a pretty place."

I pointed at Delton. "Del here went to Lookoff

59

Point this evening. That's one of his places to go think."

"It is?" Delton said stupidly. "I go somewhere to *think?*"

I shot him a daggered stare.

"Oh, yeah." Delton recovered quickly. "That's right. I go up to Lookoff Point to think. I think about all kinds of stuff. Like why is the world orange? Why are oranges colored round?" He paused, then quickly added. "Something like that anyway."

"Del says he saw you by a big boulder, Dr. McP. He says you were checking it out."

Dr. McPherson smiled. "Aye, I was looking at a large rock. On my family search."

"I'm just asking because I found a big boulder just off The Stroll with the weirdest carving on it. There was an arrow scratched on it. That wouldn't be the same rock by any chance, would it?"

"A rock with an arrow, you say? Yes, I found it. It may indeed be the very same rock."

"I found it first!" Delton blurted. "You can't have anything because I found it before you! It's mine!"

60

chapter 7

Dr. McPherson's chin dropped in shocked surprise. "Beg your pardon, laddie. What's all yours?"

"I found the treasure, so it's all mine."

Dr. McPherson became suddenly excited. "Treasure? Auck, most fascinating. Could you show me what you found?"

"Delton's jumping the gun on the treasure thing," I told him. "Delton thinks he may have found a hole that was dug some time ago."

"Where is this hole then? I was looking all day and found no hair or trace of any diggings. It has to be a short distance from the boulder. The thieves wouldn't have had time to travel too far. They would have buried the Buford's clock close to the arrow rock."

I blinked in confusion. "Thieves?"

Delton furrowed his eyelids. "The Bufords?

61

Francine's family? What have the Bufords got to do with Hole's ~~T~~reasure?"

The Scotsman sat down on a chair and dabbed his forehead again. "I think we need to talk. Then you'll understand I want nothing to do with Hole's Treasure. I'm here to check the facts in Andrew McPherson's letter."

"Andrew McPherson? Who the heck is Andrew McPherson?" Delton asked.

"He was the brother of the late Agnes," Dr. McP replied.

I put two and two together. "Agnes McPherson? Captain Hole's fiancée?"

Dr. McPherson nodded. "Andrew was a stone mason. In those days a stone mason was a builder. When he was twenty years old, Andrew came to Pirate Cove to help build his sister's mansion on the island. After his sister died and Captain Hole stopped building, Andrew went back to Scotland."

"How do you know all this?" Delton wanted to know.

As soon as my buddy finished asking the question, I knew the answer. "You're related to Andrew and Agnes, aren't you, sir?"

Dr. McP filled in the details. "That I am. I'm the great-grandson of Andrew."

The dentist pulled several sheets of folded paper from the back pocket of his pants and handed them to me. When I unfolded them, I saw they were photocopies of what appeared to be a handwritten letter. Delton shifted and peered over my shoulder.

"What is it?" Delton asked.

"A little while back, I was sorting through some old trunks in the attic of my home," Dr. McP answered. "I found a journal written by the late Agnes. Pressed between two of the pages was the original of the note you have in your hands. It's a letter sent to Agnes by her brother, Andrew, from Pirate Cove, a little over a hundred years ago. If you read it boys, you'll know why I took a little detour from the convention in Boston and came to Pirate Cove for a couple of days."

"Read it out loud, Garrett," Delton urged. "What's the letter say?"

I began to read:

April 17
Gentle Sister,

I am pleased to report that your new home goes most well. We are ahead of where we thought we would be, as we are now placing foundation stones for the playhouse. You will be most pleased when you sail here in the autumn. Captain Hole speaks of you all the time and there is no doubt he loves you with all his heart and soul. The wedding will be a wondrous event.

63

You asked in a past letter to tell you of some of my adventures in America. I replied that I had none. All I did was labor on your house, attend church, and sleep. Well, those words are now incorrect. This Sunday last, I had the most exciting adventure of my life. And, I must add, the most frightening adventure too.

But fear not, dear Agnes, for I am completely safe and unhurt. In fact, I am quite pleased with myself for everywhere I go people are calling me a hero!

It all started, when after church, I decided to sail up the mainland, find a fine spot to land, and take a walk in the thick woods. I packed a small lunch of bread and some cheese.

Before leaving, I checked the pocket of my tweed vest to make sure I had my pocket knife. I wanted to whittle myself a flute, like I used to make for you when we were children.

I purchased the knife in Boston when I first arrived in America. It has a polished brass handle. I had it initialed A.M. for my name.

The Captain has a small boat named Little Red, which is used for running chores. The paint is a soft pink color. I suppose, at one time, the boat was a bright red, hence the craft's name.

I rowed a half hour north from Pirate Cove until I landed on a pebble beach which gave way to a gentle hill into the woods. I walked up the hill, sat against a large boulder, and ate my lunch.

My curiosity was fired when I found an arrow carved upon the rock. I wondered who had made the arrow and why.

I was halfway through a tasty piece of cheese when I heard a voice in the trees to my left. For a moment my imagination flew wildly and I wondered if it was the ghost of Herman The Hermit.

Do you remember my last letter when I told you the tragic tale of Herman, the lost soul who once lived alone in a hut in the forest outside of Pirate Cove?

I cautiously peeked around the boulder.

What I saw was a ragged-looking man, dragging a large oak box toward a dug out pit, not more than twenty feet away from me. He could not have been more than a year past my own age. His clothes were grubby and looked to be a size away from his needs.

Something told me I should not announce my presence.

"Why couldn't them Bufords have had lighter stuff to steal?" he grunted to himself.

The Bufords are a founding family here in

65

Pirate Cove and very well-off. Their house was broken into just the week before. The cowards had stolen an antique clock. The clock, Captain Hole has told me, is made from pure gold.

I began to back down the gentle hill when I felt a strong hand grip my shoulder.

"You picked the wrong people to spy on!" a rough voice barked.

I turned to find an older man of huge size. He too was untidy and it was obvious he hadn't had access to a bath for weeks. He raised a gnarled stick above his shoulder and brought it down on my head.

I was knocked out cold.

Fortunately, dear sister, the blow did no permanent injury, although when I awoke my head rang like thunder. After my mind cleared, I found I was leaning back against the rock with the carved arrow.

My ankles were tied with ropes. My wrists were tied in front of me in a similar fashion. The two men stood a few yards away.

"He's awake," the younger man said. He moved closer and I could smell a blend of sweat and whisky. "What's your name?" he demanded.

I didn't answer.

"I don't really care," the man concluded. The icy calm in his voice sent shivers down

my spine. But I did my best not to show my fear.

"I just got another idea where to hide the clock," the large man said.

"What about him?" the younger man replied.

"He'll be fine right where he is," his friend answered. "He can't go far with those ropes on him. We'll decide what to do with him when we return. Maybe we should make sure he sleeps with the fish tonight."

The two men laughed for many seconds. And with that they thumped off into the trees.

I knew I didn't have long. They would soon be back. So I tried to free myself. After several minutes of pulling and twisting at the ropes on my hands, I knew I could not squirm out. I would have to think of a new plan.

Just then it came to me. My new pocket knife!

I could cut through the ropes! I reached my fingers into my vest pocket and felt the knife there. I fumbled it from my pocket, and with great effort, for my wrists were indeed tightly bound, I opened it and began to cut through the ropes. It only took a minute before my hands and ankles were free.

I stood carefully and looked around. I was unable to see the men. I did notice the pit where the younger one had dragged the chest was now empty.

Not wishing to be caught again, I sprinted down the hill toward my boat. I stumbled and tripped on the rocky beach, but reached Little Red, *untied her and pushed out to sea. I rowed into the ocean's inviting freedom.*

I went into town and took my story to the police. They caught the foolish men within the hour. But they found no hint of the clock. When questioned where they had buried their ill-gotten gains, they gave no answers.

As I write this, the Buford's gold clock has yet to be found. But because they did not have the time to travel far and dig a deep pit, they must have dug a shallow hole near the boulder. The police believe this too, although a thorough search of the area around the rock has revealed nothing.

In my haste to escape I dropped my knife. I have returned to look for it several times but cannot locate the item which saved my life.

It was a truly amazing adventure and I still shudder to think what might have happened if I had not escaped.

You are in my thoughts often, my sister, and I cannot wait until I next see you.

Your brother,
Andrew

"So you see, laddies," Dr. McPherson said when I finished reading. "I'm not at all interested in Hole's Treasure."

I stared at my buddy and he stared back.

"Do you think what you found could have anything to do with this letter, Del?" I asked.

"No," he answered. "I found Hole's Treasure."

"Maybe you didn't," I said. "Maybe it's where the thieves buried the Buford's clock."

"If you boys show me your discovery, laddies, I may be able to answer that question." Dr. McPherson said.

Delton shook his head. "I don't think so. No offense, sir, but I don't know you. You may take the treasure."

Mr. McP held up his right hand. "I have no intention of taking anything, lads. Whatever you've found is yours. I'm just curious, that's all. I've come a long way to find out if my great-grandfather's adventure has a tidy ending."

Del continued to shake his head.

"Come on, Del," I said. "Dr. McP has to go back to Boston tomorrow. You can trust him. Besides, if you don't share, you lose your hair."

"I'm already sharing," Del said. "With you."

Dr. McPherson spoke directly to Delton. "I honestly do not want what you've found, boy. I cross my heart and hope to die."

"You cross your heart?" Delton said. "You really mean that?"

"It's . . . it's . . . what I said." Dr. McP muttered. The plump Scotsman had said the expression as a figure of speech. He had no way of knowing how superstitious my friend was. Crossing your heart was a big deal to Del. Once you crossed your heart you were definitely telling the truth.

"Okay," Delton agreed. "Since you crossed your heart."

Dr. McP smiled. "This is a fine adventure. A fine, fine adventure."

chapter 8

After our talk, Dr. McPherson went up to his room, First Floor Front.

"So, that's a major surprise, huh?" I asked Delton.

Before he got the chance to answer, Gram rushed in, her face etched with worry.

"Hornbeck has had an accident," she announced.

"Hornbeck is hurt? What happened?"

"He fell off the toilet," Gram answered.

"Hornbeck fell off the toilet?" Delton puzzled. "How does somebody fall off the toilet?"

"Remember this is my accident prone little brother," I told Delton. "Is he okay, Gram? Did he do damage to the bruise on his tush?"

"He hurt his wrist," Gram informed us.

Hornbeck's wrist was swollen twice its size. I didn't need a medical degree to figure he'd

71

wrecked something. He was weepy, but I admired the way he didn't let loose with major tears.

"I'm impressed at how brave you're being, Bro," I told Hornbeck. Then to Gram, "I'll call from the Bortowski's and see how everything is later."

"Poop deck," Gram said. "No, you won't, Garrett Hawgood. Your brother needs you. No ifs, ands or buts."

"Awww," I complained.

"You are going to help me," Gram ordered. "Family emergencies come before kissy-face."

"Kissy-face?" Delton asked.

So, Delton went to Butcher's party alone while Gram drove Hornbeck, and me, as the unnecessary nurse helper, to Dr. Jenkins. The doc told us we'd have to go to Bay of Bays.

Bay of Bays has the closest hospital to Pirate Cove. It's a half hour drive if you're a tourist, twenty minutes if you're a local and know the curves and bends. By the time we got there, did the x-ray thing which showed Hornbeck had cracked his ulna bone, filled out insurance forms, waited while they put on a cast, drove back to Pirate Cove, gave the little guy pain pills and got him settled in bed, Butcher's party was over.

Which, by that time, didn't really upset me.

Part of me was anxious to see Stacey again. Maybe dance a few slow songs with her. But as I realized on the drive back from Bay of Bays, I wouldn't be able to enjoy it. My thoughts were still laying a major guilt trip on my conscience.

Stacey liked me because I'd lied; I'd told everyone Hornbeck's embarrassment was mine. I was going to have to do something about it. But what? I couldn't tell her the truth. I'd turn from Mr. Sensitive into Mr. Jerk instantly.

I had a hard time falling asleep. Which isn't surprising considering the day I'd had. Hornbeck's wrist. Lying at Butcher's party. Delton's discovery, whatever it was. Dr. McPherson and his great-grandfather's letter.

Then I remembered something from Andrew McPherson's letter. When he first heard the voice he thought it might belong to the ghost of Herman The Hermit.

Herman The Hermit?

Herman The Hippie?

That's why it had sounded familiar when Stacey told me she was a hippie called Herman in her former life. I recalled Mom telling me some kind of story about Herman The Hermit. What was it?

Hard as I tried, I couldn't remember any of the details.

I smiled to myself. Stacey thinks she used to be a hippie named Herman. She was so completely weird. I liked her so much.

I woke up early the next morning, excited to get to the woods and start digging. I showered, dressed, and was surprised to find Hornbeck munching cornflakes in the kitchen.

"How are you?" I asked. "Kind of early for you to get up. The pain in your wrist wake you?"

He studied the cast on his left arm. "It sort of pounds like it's being hit with a little hammer."

"That's your heartbeat. Because your arm's swollen you feel the blood going through. Mr. Fitzgerald told us that in Health. Say, Hornbeck, with all the running around we did last night, I never got a chance to ask you how you fell off the toilet."

"I leaned over for the toilet paper," he explained. "When I pulled it, the roll started rolling and pretty soon there was a whole bunch of toilet paper on the floor. Has that ever happened to you?"

"It's happened to everyone," I assured him.

"I bent over to roll it back up. All of a sudden I slipped off. I landed on my hands. That's how come I broke my wrist. It was real embarrassing. Gram heard me yell out. She came in and found me. My pants were still pulled down."

"She's your grandmother," I pointed out. "There's nothing to be embarrassed about. Grandmas have seen everything there is to see."

"Everything?"

"Everything."

"If you say so. When am I going to grow out of being so clumsy?"

74

"Well, now you've cracked a bone, that's almost like breaking a bone, I officially declare your accident stage over. Mine ended when I broke my nose."

My answer appeared to make him happy.

"Hey, Hornbeck, do the third graders ever talk about us eighth graders?"

"Talk about you?"

"Do you ever look at Butcher and say, 'Wow, is he big' or look at Delton and say, 'His hair is really frizzy?' You know, stuff like that?"

He chomped a spoonful of cereal. "I guess we do."

"And when the third graders talk about me, what do they say?"

"I don't think anybody's ever talked about you."

"Oh, so they don't say, 'That Garrett is a nerd.'"

Hornbeck made a serious face. "Nobody would ever call you a nerd because they know I'd get mad."

I thought about that. "Do you think they'd call me a nerd if they knew you wouldn't get mad?"

"You're talking stupid," Hornbeck declared. "I got a question for you, Garrett. How do you kiss a girl?"

"How do you . . . what? Kiss a girl? Why are you asking me that?"

"Because I need to know."

"Why do you need to know?"

"Because I've got a girlfriend."

"You've got a girlfriend? Who?"

"Nicole Olsen."

"Nicole Olsen? Michelle's sister?"

He nodded.

"The kid whose nose is always running?"

He nodded again. "On Wednesday, in gym, she threw a bean bag in my face."

"You've lost me," I told him. "She threw a bean bag in your face, so now she's your girlfriend?"

"She said she did it to get me to notice her," he explained.

"A bean bag in the face would certainly get my attention."

"Then Nicole said she was in love with me and she asked me to be her boyfriend, so I said okay."

"Why? Do you like her?"

"She laughs funny. I like that."

"I don't think I've ever heard Nicole Olsen's laugh."

"She sort of sucks her laughs through her nose, so she sounds like a pig. Her laugh sounds like a wet oink." Hornbeck tried to imitate Nicole's chuckles. "*Spl-oink. Spl-oink.*"

"Gross me out. Stop that."

"So how do you kiss a girl, Garrett?"

"Why do you want to kiss a girl who laughs like a pig?"

"She asked me to. Yesterday as we were leaving school, she said, 'Now that you're my boyfriend, I want you to kiss me. Come over to my house tomorrow and we'll watch TV and you can kiss me.' "

"Just like that?"

"Yeah."

"They must be making third graders different nowadays. Listen, Hornbeck, there's no law which says you have to kiss your girlfriend. Especially in the third grade."

He wasn't about to take my advice. "So how do I kiss a girl?" he asked for the third time.

"Well, Hornbeck, I . . . I don't really know. The truth is I've never had a girlfriend. So I've never really kissed a girl. Except for Mom and Gram and Aunt Rene."

"So I kiss her like I kiss Gram?"

I shook my head. "No. Even though I've never done it, I've seen enough movies to know kissing your girlfriend is a lot different than kissing your grandmother."

"How?"

"Well, you hold it longer for one thing. And I think you press a little bit harder. Not much. Just a little. You hold your breath. You close your eyes. And you have to move your lips a bit."

"How do you move your lips?"

"I'm not sure. I told you I haven't done it. But I think it's something like this." I twitched my lips in a slow pucker.

Hornbeck stared at me as if I'd lost my mind.

"That looks stupid, Garrett. You look like a goldfish."

"It doesn't matter what it looks like. Nicole won't be looking at your lips, will she?"

"I suppose. How long am I supposed to kiss for?"

"Until you need to breathe, I guess."

"Okay, when I'm about to pass out, I stop kissing. Is there anything else I should know about kissing, Garrett?"

"Yeah, but you don't have to worry about it in the third grade. Just remember, kiss longer, a little bit harder, don't breathe and move your lips a bit."

He finished his bowl of cornflakes, got down from the table, placed the dirty dishes in the dishwasher and announced, "I'm going to go practice kissing."

"I don't think kissing is something you can practice alone."

"I'm going to try."

"Okay. Can I give you a bit of brotherly advice?"

"What?"

"Maybe you should think real hard before you kiss a girl who always has a runny nose."

"She wipes it every once in a while."

"Oh, how exciting!"

"Huh?"

"Something I heard someone say," I told Horn-beck. "Carry on, Bro."

He did.

I made myself a mess of scrambled eggs, ate breakfast, and read a chapter of *The Things*.

Dr. McPherson interrupted my reading a half hour later.

"Good morning, sir," I greeted. "Sit down and I'll make some coffee. Gram should be down in a few minutes. She'll whip up her pancakes and sausage with maple syrup."

Dr. McPherson sat and pointed at the box of cornflakes. "No coffee, my boy. No sausage. Just some cereal, thank you."

I got a spoon, a bowl and the milk.

"Your brother, how is he today?"

"He says his arm throbs a little. Other than that he seems fine."

"Auck, good. I saw him in the sitting room, holding a cushion and kissing it. What's that all about then? Is that a normal thing for American children to do?"

"For Hornbeck it is." I told Dr. McPherson about Nicole Olsen's request.

"Ah, yes. Young love. I remember it well." He helped himself to some cereal. "Maybe you should call Delton, Garrett. After I finish breakfast, I'd like to see what you've found before I catch the bus back to Boston."

chapter 9

Delton and I sat on a large log in the clearing and watched Dr. McPherson check the indentation in the ground. He'd spent the last five minutes studying the entire area.

"I had a hard time falling asleep last night," I said.

"Me too," Delton said as he clutched his shovel. "I kept thinking about what's buried there. I mean, if it's Hole's Treasure, everything is cool. But what if it's a gold clock stolen from Francine's family, then do I get to keep it? Finders keepers, losers weepers. Still, it wouldn't be mine, would it? You should have brought your shovel. How come you didn't bring a shovel?"

"I told you I don't know where it is. I'll ask Gram when she wakes up." That was true, even though I was pretty sure I'd find the shovel if I looked in the tool shed. I think I hadn't searched because I wanted to hear Dr. McPherson's opinion first. I didn't want to feel stupid if the low spot turned out to be something natural.

Dr. McPherson joined us. "Well, I don't think it has anything to do with Andrew's letter, laddies. We're too far from the arrow rock and, if that low spot in the ground is a pit, it's much too big. The thieves wouldn't have had the time to come this far and dig so big a hole."

Delton smiled. "All right. That means it's the Captain's Treasure."

"Indeed, maybe it is," Dr. McP agreed.

And for the first time, I realized that maybe Delton's wild theory could be right. Maybe he had found Hole's Treasure. Maybe my buddy was on the verge of becoming very rich. And since he had to share or lose his hair, maybe I was about to get rich too.

"So go get your shovel and let's dig, Garrett," Delton suggested.

"It's none of my business," Dr. McPherson said. "But perhaps you shouldn't be so hasty."

"What do you mean?" Delton asked suspiciously.

"Maybe you should tell the police authorities first," Dr. McP instructed. "You see, I did a little checking before visiting here. Apparently, it's best to have a permit before you look for treasure."

"A permit?" I asked. "You mean like a license?"

"I was told you need permission from the Maine government," our guest stated.

"So, what if we don't?" Delton asked. "Who's going to know?"

"The permit would be protection for you," Dr. McP pointed out. "It proves you found the treasure first and no one else can claim it. And you may need an archeologist to supervise the digging. If there's anything the state thinks is historically important, that is."

"Geez," I said. "It sure is complicated."

"My advice would be to tell your Gram, Garrett. You're going to need an adult to get the permit." He checked his watch. "But like I said, it's none of my business. You boys are going to have to decide what to do. I have to go pack now." He pulled out his wallet and removed a couple of business cards, which he handed to us. "Do me a favor, laddies. Drop me a line and tell me if you find something. And if you ever hear anything about the details in Andrew's letter, I'd appreciate a note about that too. Perhaps I'll see you before I catch the bus. If not, good-bye, boys." He shook our hands and walked back toward The Stroll.

"So what do you think?" Del asked when Dr. McP was out of sight. "Do we wait until I get a permit?"

"I don't think you have a choice," I answered. "You don't want anyone else taking Hole's Treasure just because you didn't get a license to dig, do you?"

"You're right." His voice was heavy with disappointment. "It sure would have been fun finding those treasure chests ourselves though. But, I guess I can wait if I end up rich."

We continued to sit on the log, both of us frustrated by what Dr. McPherson had told us. Yet, at the same time, we were both excited by his opinion that the sunken square, if it was a hole, was too far and too big to have been dug by the thieves Andrew McPherson had met. As each second passed, I was a little more convinced Delton may really have found Hole's Treasure.

"Oh, Stacey says hello," Delton said. "When she found out you had to take Hornbeck to Bay of Bays, and wouldn't be back for the party, she told me she wants you to call her this morning."

"She does? Why?"

"I don't know. But she came up to me three different times and said, 'Get Garrett to call me tomorrow morning.' I think she likes you a lot."

I heard something in the trees behind Delton, something like branches being pushed aside. I looked over Delton's shoulder into a bushy part of the forest. My buddy twisted around to see what I was looking at.

"Did you see something?" he asked.

"No, I thought I heard something."

I stood up, walked over and elbowed some bush branches aside. Delton imitated me, brushing

83

branches to one side with his shovel. We saw nothing that wasn't supposed to be there.

"There's nothing," Delton said. "Maybe it was a deer. Or some kind of bird."

"Yeah, maybe."

We walked back to the log and sat down.

"So tell me about the party, Del. Was it fun?"

"It was great. We danced a bit. Butcher kept grossing everybody out by shoving snacks up his nose."

"No way."

"The boy never fails to amaze," Delton said. "Do you know he can fit five peanuts in his right nostril and four in his left nostril?"

"It's lucky he didn't get them stuck."

"He just blew them back into the bowl. Naturally, no one at the party wanted to eat peanuts after that."

"Disgusting."

"No, disgusting was when Baker came in looking for a snack and pickcd up the bowl of peanuts and started gorfing them before anybody could say anything. Finished them off in a few seconds."

"Don't tell me any more. How'd you get on with Francine?"

"I walked her home. I kissed her good-night."

I punched his arm. "Way to go, good buddy."

"Ow." He rubbed his muscle.

"What was the kiss like, Del? What did you do?"

"We kissed."

"How?"

"We just kissed."

"For how long?"

"A couple of seconds maybe."

"Did you kiss a little . . . you know, harder than when you kiss your mom?"

"I guess. I didn't really think about it."

"Think about it now."

"It wasn't harder. It was more gentle."

"Did you close your eyes?"

"I think so. I don't remember."

"You were inches away from her face. She'd be out of focus. How can you not remember an out-of-focus Francine?"

He shrugged. "I suppose I was concentrating on the kiss."

"Did you move your lips when you kissed her?"

"Move my lips?"

"Like this." I did my goldfish imitation.

Delton stared at me in disbelief.

"Did you move your lips like that?"

"No, I didn't do that. Why?"

"I'm just trying to figure, how *do* you kiss a girl?"

When we got back to Bed & Roses, Delton went home with shovel in hand and I headed into the kitchen. When I walked in, Gram was clearing off the table.

"Oh, there you are, Garrett," Gram said. "You were up early this morning. I heard you in the bathroom at dawn."

"I couldn't fall asleep."

"And Hornbeck was up early too. He says his wrist doesn't hurt too much."

"Those pain pills must really work," I noted.

"Maybe they work too well. Maybe we shouldn't give him another pill. A few minutes ago, I caught him acting strangely. I walked past your room and he was kissing the dresser mirror. Imagine that? He had his eyes closed and was kissing himself in the mirror."

Gram waited for me to react. When I didn't, she said, "You don't find that odd behavior, Garrett?"

"He's just rehearsing," I said. "He's practicing to do some serious kissy-face."

"What?" I could have sworn Gram's eyebrows almost touched her hairline. "Hornbeck? Kissy-face? What do you mean?"

"Maybe you should ask him yourself, Gram. Then try to talk him out of it. The girl he wants to kiss always has wet stuff running out of her nose."

"Wet stuff? That makes me feel ill."

"That's my opinion too. But Hornbeck likes her laugh. She sounds like a pig with nasal congestion."

"What exactly are you talking about, Garrett Hawgood?"

86

"Talk to Hornbeck." I opened the fridge and helped myself to a glass of orange juice. "Listen, there's something big I've got to tell you, Gram. Something I was going to keep a secret until Delton and I actually dug something up. But things are different now. You see, yesterday Delton needed a lucky pinecone from Lookoff Point and on his way back he had to pee and now I think we need you to get us a permit . . ."

Gram was so stunned when I finished telling her about Delton's find, she spent minutes wandering around the kitchen, tidying things that were already tidy, and mumbling, "Oh, my. Oh, my. This is so hard to believe. Maybe it's Hole's Treasure? So hard to believe." Then she started asking, over and over, if I was joking. "Are you sure you're not fooling me, Garrett?"

I don't think she really believed me until Dr. McPherson came downstairs with his suitcase and confirmed our discovery. Then Gram spent the next half hour surfing through the house, once again tidying things that were already tidy, and mumbling "Oh, my. Oh, my. This is so hard to believe. Hole's Treasure? So hard to believe."

When she finally sat down for a cup of tea, I asked her about something which had been bugging me since last night. "Gram, maybe you can help me refresh my memory. When I was little, I think Mom told me a story about someone who lived around Pirate Cove. Someone called Herman The Hermit. Do you know anything about that?"

Gram's face fell into a relaxed smile. "I certainly do. Your grandfather, bless his soul, would tell your mother all about Herman when she was a girl. Herman The Hermit was a loner who lived in the woods around Pirate Cove a long, long time ago. Your grandfather used to know the place where his hut used to be. He took your mother there a few times. Course, there was nothing left to see. Apparently, some boys burned it down after Herman passed away."

"Okay, now I think I remember. Mom told me something about how Grandpa would take her and her friends to go see . . . what?" The memory was so dim, I couldn't remember. "What did they go visit?"

"I don't know. I didn't tramp through the woods with them. I had your Aunt Rene to take care of."

"Do you have any idea how this Herman guy died, Gram?"

"All the stories say he fell off Lookoff Point. Fell onto the rocks below," Gram answered.

That was strange. Stacey told me Herman The Hippie fell off a cliff too. What a coincidence.

"Are there ghost stories about him?"

"When I was young, there were tales of how his ghost still guarded the belongings he'd hidden in the forest. Silly stories."

"This is fascinating, Gram."

"Herman made marks on trees all over the forest," Gram finished. "Marks leading to his hut. When he was young, Grandpa knew where some of the marked trees were."

"I wish I could have known Grandpa," I said. "I think I would have liked him a whole lot."

"And I know he would have liked you too," Gram said. "He would be very proud of you. Finding Hole's Treasure? Imagine that."

I walked Dr. McPherson to the bus stop outside the Pirate Cove Cafe and waited for the Greyhound with him. He speculated, "If that is Captain Hole's Treasure like you think, you boys may be very rich."

"That would be nice," I said. "The more I think about it, the more I think it could be the treasure. But part of me knows it's still a long shot."

He shook my hand again. "I'm delighted to have met you, young man. Perhaps you'll be able to visit Scotland some day. If you do, I'll be glad to take you on a long walk across the Highlands."

"And maybe you can come back to Pirate Cove for a longer visit," I said.

After the bus left, I had the feeling I was going to meet our dentist guest again.

"Now, to go see what the lovely Stacey wants," I said to myself.

chapter 10

I went to the Bortowski house to speak to Stacey. Baker answered the door and went to the
guest room to get her. He returned fifteen seconds later.

"Stacey says she'll be out in a minute," Baker
told me.

"Thanks. Is Butcher home?" I wanted to thank
him for inviting me to his party, even though I
had to leave early.

"Butcher ain't here," Baker answered. "He left
real early to go dig clams."

"Clams? I didn't know Butcher dug clams."

"Butcher does a lot of dumb stuff. He took a
couple of shovels to go dig clams. You want to
make a federal case out of it?"

"I just . . . forget it. I'll see him later."

"Hey, Garrett, will you vote on something? I
got this bet with my brother. I say dog food tastes
better if you eat it with a knife and fork. He says

it tastes better if you eat it with your fingers. What do you think?"

"I, er . . ." I studied the little guy. This had to be a joke. So I went along. "It depends. Are you talking about dry dog food or canned dog food? There's a big diff."

Little Baker appeared suddenly confused. "I was talking about the canned stuff. You think maybe Butcher is talking about the kibble stuff?" He turned and headed toward the kitchen. "Hey, Mom," he shouted. "Do we have any kibble?"

Maybe he wasn't joking. I shuddered at the thought.

Travis Bowman appeared in the hallway. "Hi, Garrett. My sister is changing her clothes for the umpteenth time. She wants to wear something that will impress you."

I liked the thought of that.

"How's Hornbeck? Stacey said he busted his arm last night."

"He cracked a bone."

"Decent."

"Stacey is changing her clothes to impress me?"

"Yeah, she's putting on her hippie stuff. I wish she'd stop being so weird. I wish she'd go back to being like she was before we got to Pirate Cove."

"Stacey is different now?" I wondered out loud.

"Yeah, last week she was normal. As soon as she got to Pirate Cove she started talking about being different and reading hornyscopes and she started drinking fridge water and dressing dumb. And liking you. Why would anyone like you?"

"Watch it," I replied. "Or else."

"I know, underwear yank. Well, go ahead and try it 'cause I'm not wearing any underwear today."

"You're not . . . why aren't you wearing underwear?"

"So you can't wedgie me. And if you want to learn what Stacey wrote about you in her diary last night, you'll have to pay me ten bucks."

"You read your sister's diary?"

He nodded.

"That's awful. Diaries are supposed to be private."

"You sound like you should go on Sesame Street, Garrett," the little twerp mocked. "She didn't say, 'Don't read it,' and she leaves it around, so I figure it's fair game."

"That's not ethical."

"I don't know what that means. Give me ten bucks and I'll tell you what she wrote."

"No way."

"Five bucks."

"Travis, I'm not going to pay you anything. It's none of my business."

"Three bucks."

"A dollar," I countered.

"Two. And that's my final offer."

"Okay." I took out my wallet and handed him

two singles. Had I lost my mind? "You sure you're only eight years old?"

He shoved the bills into his pants pocket. "Stacey wrote that she wants to go somewhere alone with you so she can kiss you. And Stacey wants to show you her mole."

"Her mole?"

"Yeah, that's what she wrote. I'm going to go visit Hornbeck and check out his cast."

"Wait a sec. What mole?"

Travis zipped out the door.

"Do you mean the mole Baker saw in the bathroom?" By the time I got the sentence out, Travis was out of hearing range.

"Hi, Garrett." Stacey appeared in the hallway. She was dressed in her faded, ripped blue jeans and a stars-and-stripes T-shirt. Around her waist was a thick, multicolored belt made out of what looked like colored rope. Her long hair was tied back in a ponytail. I thought she was a vision of beauty. I'm not sure where I heard someone on a TV show refer to a girl as *a vision of beauty,* but it sure fit at that moment.

"Hi, Stacey. Delton told me you wanted me to call you. I was down by the cafe and I thought I'd drop by."

"I knew you were coming. I think I have a slight sense of clairvoyance. I sense the ripples of time in the universe, feel the tugs of the future. I must check my horoscope later, Garrett. You're

93

an Aries and I think there must be an Aries in my Romance House today."

"I'm glad." And I was. Even though I had no idea what she was talking about, being in my favorite girl's Romance House sounded like a good place to be. "You look great today. That's a neat belt."

"It's from the Loranu Islands in the South Pacific," she said. "Actually, it's a twenty-four-foot piece of woven string. Young people on Loranu twist it around their waists if they're looking for a mate."

I didn't have a clue what I should say about that, so I said, "Would you like to go for a walk, Stacey?"

She smiled. "I'd like that very much."

It took twenty minutes for Stacey and me to travel on the gravel and rock beach between Big Dock and Little Dock. I could probably run the same stretch in under two minutes. But we weren't interested in covering the distance quickly.

We were interested in spending time with each other.

We talked about all kinds of things: school, her famous father and his new book, how her brother was getting used to Pirate Cove, whether the autumnal equinox should be made a national holiday, how beautiful the beach looked.

When the beach turned to sand near Little

Dock, we stopped and looked out at Hole's Island and the ocean for the longest time.

"I get kind of mushy when I look out at the ocean," Stacey told me. "It's so beautiful here."

"Yeah, it is," I said. "Someday you'll have to go to Vancouver. The ocean is beautiful there too. In a different way. It's awesome to watch the sunset. It's like a giant fireball as it oozes into the Pacific."

Stacey twirled the end of her ponytail with her fingers. Yet another sweet move.

"That's so poetic," she said in a soft voice. " 'It's like a giant fireball as it oozes into the Pacific.' You have such a way with words, Garrett."

I was about to tell her, they weren't my words, that my father had once described a sunset that way to me. But I didn't.

Add another notch to my level of guilt about fibbing. I needed to tell her about the TV hugging. I needed to tell her soon.

"Do you know I've never been able to talk to a boy about horoscopes or reincarnation, or anything like that," Stacey said. "Boys just aren't interested."

"I'm interested," I told her.

"But you don't believe any of it, do you?" she stated.

How should I respond to that? She was right. I thought horoscopes were dumb. And former lives? If Stacey thought I shared one with her, so be it. But there was no way I believed it. If I told her my feelings, how would she react?

"Let's just say I don't know enough about those things yet." There, that was a diplomatic answer.

Stacey hesitated, as if she wanted to say something else. She bit her bottom lip and stared at her feet.

I tried to imitate the guys in Dennis Queen novels, the guys who say exactly the right thing at the right time. "I guess that's why I like you, Stacey. I like the things you talk about. The way you look. The way you walk. The way you play with your hair. Everything. You're so different."

She turned to face me. "I wish you wouldn't . . . Garrett, there's something I have to tell you. But first, just in case you get . . . No, I don't even want to think about that." She closed her eyes and raised her face toward me.

She wants me to kiss her, I thought. She's waiting for me to kiss her.

She leaned closer toward me.

The first thing I did was panic. But only for a second. Then I ran the instructions I'd given Hornbeck through my head. "Just hold your breath," I said to myself. "Keep kissing longer. Kiss harder. No, don't do that. Remember what Delton said? Kiss more gently. Yeah, that's it. And move your lips."

I tilted my head downward and puckered.

Wait. There was something else. What else did I need to do?

Close my eyes. That was it.

I glanced across Sandy Beach before closing my eyes and slowly inched my face closer to hers. Soon I felt the warmth of her lips on mine. So this was it. I was kissing a girl for the first time and it was just so exciting. It was . . .

Immediately, I snapped back and flared my eyelids.

Surprised, Stacey did the same thing.

"What the . . . ?" I said.

"Did I do something wrong?" Stacey asked.

I peered across Sandy Beach. Something wasn't right. But what? All I saw was an empty beach. It looked the way it always looked.

Then it hit me. Empty. Sandy Beach was empty. That was normal. It was nearly always empty after Labor Day. And that was it. It shouldn't be empty. There should be at least one person on the beach.

Butcher Bortowski should be here.

I recalled what Baker had told me at the Bortowski house. "Butcher ain't here. He left real early to go dig clams."

Sandy Beach was the only place to dig clams in Pirate Cove. And Butcher wasn't there. That meant . . . No, it couldn't be. It was impossible. Then again, it was a definite possibility. Baker said Butcher had a pair of shovels. If he wasn't digging clams, then he could be digging . . . No. Had Butcher somehow found Hole's Treasure too? I had to go check it out.

Stacey, of course, didn't know why I was having an anxiety attack. She thought it had something to do with her. "I've never kissed a boy before," Stacey said, embarrassed. "Was I doing something wrong?"

"Maybe I should go get Delton," I thought out loud. "Maybe I'm going to need Delton's help."

Stacey's embarrassment instantly turned into puzzlement. "Excuse me? You need Delton's help to kiss me?"

"Huh? No, it wasn't anything you did, Stacey. It's Butcher. I've got to find Butcher."

"You need Butcher's help to kiss me?" she half-whispered, afraid to hear my answer.

"Did Butcher say anything to you this morning?" I asked. "Anything unusual?"

"I only saw him for a few seconds. He mentioned something about dog food. I wasn't really listening."

"Anything else?"

"No, I only saw him for a few . . . Wait, he said something about coming back home with a surprise."

"Oh, no," I moaned. "Did he say what?"

"I try not to listen to my cousin," she confessed.

I had to get to the clearing pronto. I didn't have time to get Delton. I had to stop Butcher before he wrecked everything. Or before he found anything.

I planted a peck on Stacey's lips. "I've got something important to do. I'll explain later, Honey. I'll call you in a bit"

"Honey?" she asked. "You just called me Honey?"

I charged across Shore Road and into the woods.

If I could run as fast as I charged through those woods that Saturday morning, I'd be junior high state track champion, no sweat. The adrenalin pumped so fast, I virtually flew down The Stroll, my feet only skimming the ground. I reached the arrow rock in minutes. From there, I barreled through the trees, saplings and bushes toward the old oak tree.

Every so often, when I'm playing a Super NES game, I get to a point where the control pad feels like a part of my hand and I can get the game character through a level with no problem at all. And, as I zipped along for those few minutes, I felt like one of those invincible Nintendo heroes. I sprinted through the trees, dodging trunks and ducking under low branches with amazing speed. I hurdled logs and jumped stumps with incredible grace. I was on a tear.

Our visits through the woods had made a footpath of stomped grass and broken twigs between

99

the arrow rock and the massive oak. I guessed that was how Butcher found the hollow in the ground. "Even Butcher would be able to follow this," I said to myself.

Minutes later, I emerged into the giant oak tree clearing, puffing and panting. Riverlets of sweat dripped off my chin. And I immediately saw my worst fears realized. My classmate stood in the middle of the low spot, ripping shovelfuls of dirt from the ground and pitching them onto an already large pile beside the giant tree. He'd dug a hole well past his knees.

Butcher glanced at me and anger creased his face. "Oh, no, the nerd nose is here," he said out loud to nobody.

chapter 11

I walked toward Butcher with my hands on my hips, forcing my breathing under control, flashing my best icy stare. "Get out of there, Bortowski."

He ignored me, returned his attention to the pit and dug another few shovelfuls of dirt.

"I said get out of there!" I repeated. "That belongs to Del."

Butcher rammed the shovel into the ground and rested his hands on the handle. He looked at the hole for a moment. "Funny, I don't see his name anywhere."

"He found it first."

"You can't prove that. I can say I found it last week. So it's mine."

"That's not true, Butcher. You found it because you saw the path we made coming in here."

He shook his head. "Naw, I'm smarter than that. I knew something was suspicious last night

101

when my dad said something about a rock and you freaked out. I followed you when you left the party. I heard every word you and Hayes said by the boulder. You know, that wasn't too bright of you guys. Blabbing on and on about finding Hole's Treasure. If it was me, I would have kept my trap shut. That's why I deserve whatever is buried here." He tapped his forehead with his index finger. "I got a higher IQ than you and Delton put together."

"That was you Del saw in the trees last night?" I was as angry at myself as I was at Butcher. I should have checked.

"And it was me you heard here this morning when you and Hayes were talking to that fat guy. I set my alarm early and waited for you to come out of your house and followed you again." Once more, Butcher tapped his forehead. "I'm Mr. Genius."

I had to get him out of the pit. "If you heard what Dr. McPherson said, then you know the treasure is ours. My grandmother is going to get a permit to dig it. A permit in our name."

"No guff? Let's see. Correct me if I'm wrong, Baghead, but I don't think your stupid permit exists. So whatever is buried here is mine because I'm digging and you're just standing there watching me."

"Butcher," I reasoned. "It isn't fair."

He laughed, deep and from the bottom of his

gut. "Fair? Life isn't fair, Hawgood. You should know that by now. I'm here. You're not. Bye-bye."

"Get out of there!" I shouted. "Or else!"

"Or else what? Or else you're going to stop me? Go home, look at yourself in the mirror, check out what a weakling you are, and then be grateful I'm letting you go without pounding your ears into your skull."

Little pinks spots danced in front of my eyes. I heard myself sucking air through my teeth. My fists clenched. Every muscle in my body tensed. I'd never been this angry before.

Butcher returned to the chore of removing dirt from the hole.

If I had thought of my options, I obviously wouldn't have done what I did next. There were several *intelligent* things I could have done.

I could have got Delton to help me. We'd probably have ended up in a big fight. Maybe it was possible for Butcher to take out Delton and me at the same time, but it wouldn't be easy. It would sure stop him from digging.

A better plan would have been to tell Gram, ask for her help. No doubt, she'd call Mr. Bortowski and they'd come out to the clearing. They'd do something to force Butcher to stop.

Maybe the best plan would have been a call to Sheriff Carson. Explain what we'd found. Explain what Dr. McP had said about digging up something which could be historic. The sheriff would have stopped Butcher fast enough.

But I wasn't thinking about good, better and best plans. The only thing I wanted right then was to stop Butcher from scooping dirt out of our Treasure Pit. The little pink dots in my vision flowed together and soon I was looking at the world through a pink screen.

Butcher glared at me with a sneer on his face. "I told you to get lost, Garrett. You're too much of a wimp to do anything. I'm sorry I got mad at you for being with Stacey in the kitchen last night. You guys deserve each other, Miss Space Cadet and Mr. Wimp, the perfect couple."

The pink screen turned crimson red. It felt as if my head was going to explode.

"Aaarrrggghhh!" I screamed as I lowered my head and charged at Butcher like a raptor with rabies.

I admit to being a bit cautious, at times. Okay, I'll even say a bit *wimpy,* on rare occasions. But in that fraction of time, I'd transformed into a human battering ram. I bashed my shoulder full force into Butcher's chest.

And I discovered the answer to that physics question: What happens when an irresistible force meets an immovable object?

The answer is: Misery! Major anguish!

When we connected, I heard a loud explosion. I don't think it was the sound of our bodies colliding. I'm pretty sure it was the noise my brain made as it squashed into one half my skull.

Butcher staggered off-balance, dropped to his knees, and made the funniest groaning noise. I swayed above him, trying to refocus. After the longest time, Butcher fumbled back to his feet. We wobbled in front of each other for a few seconds.

"Are you nuts?" Butcher wheezed.

"I want you out of here," I wheezed back.

I wound back, ready to take a roundhouse punch to the side of his head, but Butcher reached out and grabbed my hand. His palm covered my fist like a catcher's mitt.

"Why are you trying to fight me? You know I can cream you anytime." In one smooth motion, he lazily swung his other hand around and popped me in the gut.

To give Butcher credit, he didn't cuff me with his fist; he whacked me with the flat of his hand. And he didn't do it all that hard, more like a quick snap than a punch.

But it was hard enough. The air rushed out of me and I fell back to the ground like a sack of cement. The pain was a fence post in my intestines. I lay, face-first, flat out in the hole Butcher had dug. I tried to suck in some air.

"Why would you do that, Hawgood?" Butcher raved above me. "You got a death wish? I was giving you a hard time to make you go away. I

105

didn't want to hurt you. Why would you want to hurt me?"

I couldn't say anything. I was still trying to get some air into my lungs. I think I was about to pass out. The redness had gone from my vision. Now I was seeing things through a tunnel.

I managed to get a little air. Then a little more. Still more. At last, a breath. I coughed a few times. Another breath. This time I sucked some dirt into my mouth. My eyesight slowly returned to normal. The pain became a bearable ache.

Butcher still couldn't believe I'd attacked him. "What got into you, Garrett?"

I looked at the dirt a few inches in front of my face. Nice, dark sandy-brown, northern Maine soil. Then I noticed something darker. Something almost black.

With great effort, I heaved myself to my knees and brushed at the dirt. The ground got darker. It got darker because I was brushing the dirt off the top of something. Soon, I'd cleaned an area the size of my hand and I knew what the dark stuff was.

Wood. Old wood painted with tar.

"There's something here," I said.

Butcher grabbed the back of my T-shirt and with one violent jerk he yanked me to my feet. "Let me see," he ordered. He kicked at the exposed wood with his foot, removing more of the dirt.

"It could be the top of a wooden chest," I guessed.

"Could be," Butcher agreed. He reached down and picked up his shovel. "I got another shovel over by the tree. Go get it and help me."

I reached for the second shovel, then hesitated. "What about what Dr. McPherson said? We shouldn't dig because there may be something here that's history."

Butcher ignored my objection and madly attacked the ground with his shovel.

"We should wait," I suggested.

He didn't stop digging. "The way I see it, Hawgood, you can't stop me. So you either help or you don't."

That was all the excuse I needed. I was suddenly so overcome with curiosity and excitement about finally finding Hole's Treasure that I told myself Butcher was correct.

There *was* no way I could stop him. Other than banging him over the head with the other shovel which, I must admit, was a thought which passed through my brain. But only for a nanosecond. Second degree murder was not an option.

And so with the thought, *if you can't beat 'em, join 'em,* running through my head, I reached for the second shovel and with a gusto equal to Butcher's, I began to assault the dirt.

chapter 12

For a few minutes, Butcher and I were transformed into human gophers, ripping the ground in a mad fury. Butcher didn't bother to pitch the dirt onto the pile by the tree trunk anymore. He heaved and flung soil in every direction. I did the same. Thinking back on it, it's lucky we didn't crush each other's skulls with our flying shovels.

It didn't take us long to remove enough soil to realize the tarred wood wasn't the top of a chest or trunk. We uncovered several side by side pine boards, all about six inches wide and five feet long.

"They're two by sixes," Butcher said. "My old man uses them when he builds boat houses. They're wall studs."

Further scooping cleared the dirt from a total of twelve pieces of equal-sized lumber. The timber formed the foundation of the square sunken area Delton had found.

"What the heck is this?" Butcher asked. "This ain't no treasure."

"Why would somebody bury twelve boards in the middle of the forest?" I thought out loud.

I studied the last plank, the one closest to the oak tree. I jabbed it gently with the tip of my shovel. The old wood dented, but didn't chip. "This can't be a hundred years old. It's not rotten."

"That don't mean nothing," Butcher told me. "It's been painted with tar and under the ground. There's no telling how old it could be." Then he grumbled. "This ain't no treasure. This sucks."

"Maybe these boards and the arrow on the rock are a red herring," I said.

"A dead herring? What's a dead fish got to do with anything?"

"A *red* herring," I corrected. "That's what they call a clue in a mystery story which doesn't lead anywhere. Maybe Captain Hole carved the arrow to throw people off."

"Then the guy was a dork," Butcher asserted. "He's lucky he's dead or I'd slap him around."

"Then again, it doesn't make sense," I went on. "Why go to the trouble of burying twelve boards? I can't think of a reason."

In frustration, Butcher pounded the planks with his shovel. Strangely, they resonated with a bass drum-like, muffled boom.

"Huh? What's that?" Butcher puzzled.

He bashed his shovel onto the boards two more times.

Boom. Boom.

Butcher's angry sneer turned into a happy face. "It's hollow. These things are covering a hole. Maybe the treasure is right under here. Help me move them."

Using our shovels as levers, we pried the two middle planks from their resting place. Minutes later, we knew Butcher was correct. There *was* a hole under the boards. We knelt and peered into the darkness below.

"Can you see anything, Butcher?"

"Nothing," he answered.

I shifted in an attempt to let daylight into the pit. All we could see was blackness.

"Do you think it's really deep?" I asked.

Instead of answering, Butcher sniffed, like he was a dog around a fireplug, sucking loud snotty breaths. For some reason, I thought of Hornbeck's girlfriend, Nicole.

Butcher continued to snort.

"What are you doing, Butcher?"

"I smell something. I smell . . . water."

"Water? How can you smell water? Water has no smell."

"Sure it does. You can smell the ocean. The sewer lagoon. And I can smell water here."

Butcher scrambled on hands and knees, grabbed a small rock and scrambled back. He dropped the pebble into the darkness. A second later there was a loud plop.

"See," Butcher said. "Water."

"The hole must have flooded."

"I think it's something else. Let's get rid of the rest of the boards and see what we've got."

When we'd removed the other ten boards, we found ourselves standing beside a circular hole, four feet across. Now that it was open, we saw the walls were lined with smooth red bricks. The morning light reflected off the water, which was about fifteen feet below.

Again, Butcher stated the obvious. "This is a well."

Now we knew why someone had buried the twelve boards. They were covering a well. But it didn't solve the mystery. What was a well doing in the middle of nowhere?

Butcher got down on his knees again, examined our discovery for a while, then pointed to something in the hole. "Look at this."

I squatted beside him and followed the line of his index finger. He was targeting one of the bricks near the top. It was scratched with the capital letter 'H'.

"There's Captain Hole's initial," Butcher said. "Maybe you were wrong about that dead herring thing, Hawgood. Maybe the arrow is pointing to the well."

"Even if it is. Why build a well way out here?"

"Who cares?" Butcher said. "It's here. And maybe Captain Hole used this well to hide his treasure, huh? Maybe he threw his gold and stuff down there. Could be, right?"

I had one of those feelings Delton had when he saw Dr. McPherson walk from Shore Road into The Stroll. I *felt* Butcher was wrong. Captain Hole didn't have anything to do with this well. Something else was going on.

But what?

"So now I have to figure out how to get to the bottom of the well," Butcher mused. "How am I going to do that?"

"Maybe you can tie a bag of rocks around your neck and jump into the stupid well!" a voice barked.

We twisted around and watched a figure barrel across the clearing toward us.

"Delton," I said.

"Oh, no, it's the other nerd nose," Butcher mumbled to himself. "How come I never get a break?"

"Yeah, it's me, Garrett," Delton shouted. "I'm the guy who found this treasure pit. I'm the person who decided to share it with *his* best friend. Remember?"

I glanced at Butcher, then at the well. "It's not what you think, Del. I just . . ."

My buddy wasn't in the mood for rational explanations. "I knew I was in trouble when the syrup ran off the side of my waffle. It's major bad luck if the syrup flows off a waffle. Almost as soon as it happened, Stacey knocked on my door. She said she was worried because you were acting weird. She told me you'd said something about Butcher and ran off down The Stroll. She asked me if I knew where you were going."

"Stacey was worried about me?"

"I can't believe you'd do this, Garrett," Delton snarled. "I can't believe you'd tell Butcher. I can't believe you'd dig it up without me. All that talk about getting a permit was just trash. How could you do this behind my back?"

"Chill out, Hayes!" Butcher ordered. "Listen to your buddy."

"I trusted you, Garrett," Delton raved on. "I didn't know you were a liar."

"I don't lie." I thought about the TV hugging thing. "I mean, I wouldn't lie to you. Not ever."

He marched toward me with the strangest look on his face, angry and hurt at the same time. "I trusted you," he said.

I noticed tears on his cheeks.

"Del, I—"

He shoved his hands into my chest, like a blocker does to a defensive tackle. I didn't expect Delton to do anything like that and I wasn't ready for it. The force of Delton's attack knocked the air out of me and I reeled backward.

"Watch it, Hawgood!" Butcher yelled.

I felt the big guy's fingers try to grab my arm.

"Oh, no!" Delton shouted. His angry-hate expression changed to one of panic.

Delton made a move to grab me too, but I was falling out of his reach. I felt Butcher's fingers slip as I plummeted toward the ground.

Of course, there wasn't any ground for me to land on.

Only a four-foot-wide hole.

I tumbled into the well.

At this point, my memory gets fuzzy for a few seconds because I didn't drop straight down. I bashed violently into the bricks before plunging into the water. I'm not sure what part of my body collided with the wall of the well first. Perhaps it was my shoulder. Maybe it was my face. Maybe it was both at the same time. I guess, in the end, it doesn't really matter. I smacked into the well wall hard enough to knock myself senseless for a couple of seconds.

My next clear memory is one of being cold and lost in space. I was thrashing and gasping, trying to breathe, with awful pains in my right shoulder and across my face. There was an unpleasant, yet familiar, bitter taste in my mouth. I knew my eyes were open, yet everything was black. There was nothing to see. I realized I'd fallen into the well and I was under the water, but I had no idea which way was up or down.

My sweeping hands brushed something solid,

something with soft ridges that was slightly slimy.

Bricks.

"Stop moving," a voice in my head coached. It was Margo, my swimming instructor from the Y in Vancouver. I was remembering one of her lessons. "If you ever get disoriented under water," the memory of Margo said, "stop moving. You'll float to the surface. A human body will float. Just relax."

I followed Margo's advice and froze.

And slowly, I felt myself rising, bumping the bricks with my knees and elbows. Then something appeared in the darkness, a circle of murky light which gradually grew brighter.

For a fraction of a second, I had the stupid thought that maybe I was dead. I'd once read a true story about people who died on operating tables and were brought back to life. They all said that while they were unconscious they drifted toward a circle of light.

I quickly dismissed the idea when I gagged on the bitter liquid in my mouth. That light is the top of the well, I thought. I'm seeing the sky through the hole in the ground. Swim toward it.

I thrust my arms in a breast stroke and my shoulder protested in pain. I broke the surface, coughing and gasping, sucking for air.

"Are you okay-ay?" Delton's voice echoed off the bricks.

I coughed an answer and suddenly knew the source of the bitter taste.

Blood.

"You idiot, Delton!" Butcher shouted above me. "What a stupid thing to do. I should chuck you down there for being such a jerk. What if Garrett couldn't swim?" Butcher called down to me. "You *can* swim, right, Hawgood-ood?"

"Yeah," I sputtered.

Treading water with my right arm, I gingerly felt my face with my left hand. My bottom lip was split. As soon as I touched my nose and felt it slip loosely between my fingers, I felt a railway spike of pain travel through my head. I knew it was broken.

"Are you okay?" Delton repeated.

"No," I cried. "I've busted my nose and wrecked my shoulder. Wrecked it bad. I don't think I can ... I don't think I can tread water for long. The water's cold. Get me out of here."

I heard Delton above me. He was whispering to Butcher, but the brick walls amplified his words. "How are we going to get him out, Butcher?"

"Beats me," Butcher whispered back.

"Help me, guys," I groaned. "My shoulder ... I can't ... help me."

chapter 13

Every time I waved my right arm to tread water, razor-sharp pain spread from my neck to the tips of my fingers. My mouth slipped under the surface and I swallowed a mouthful of dank water mixed with blood.

"The water is freezing," I complained.

In hindsight, I was wrong. The water was cold, but it was far from freezing. It felt frigid because I was stunned. The surprise of falling into the well, added to the trauma of bashing into the bricks, had sent me into some kind of shock. And the shock cranked my senses into overdrive. What I saw, heard, felt, smelled and tasted magnified tenfold. Cold water was freezing water. Whispered words were bullhorned. Shoulder pain became body agony. Stale air turned into a musty stench. Slightly bitter blood was almost caustic.

"My shoulder hurts too much to swim," I called.

"We have to do something, Butcher," Delton whined.

"Yeah," Butcher replied. "We need a rope. Run back to town and get my old man, Delton. Tell him what's happened. He'll know what to do."

"I can't leave," Delton said. "It's my fault Garrett is down there. I've got to stay and help."

"Go get my father," Butcher ordered. "That's the help we need."

"I can't," Delton pleaded. "I have to stay here."

Butcher's head vanished from the well opening. Delton disappeared a moment later. I heard shuffling. Then Butcher's muffled voice. Then wrestling noises. Then, a couple of grunts and a few seconds of silence.

"What's going on up there?" I yelled.

Another grunt.

More seconds of silence.

Finally, Delton's face reappeared. "I'm going to get help, Garrett," he said in a squeaky voice. "You hang in, buddy."

His head was replaced by Butcher's. "Run as fast as you can move, Delton!" Butcher shouted. Then he called down to me. "Hayes and me had a little talk. He's booting it to get my father. I'm going to stay here and help you. You're going to be okay."

"Yeah, I'm going to be okay," I said, surprised how soft my voice sounded.

I knew I was lying to myself. Every time I

118

moved my shoulder, the pain hitched a notch. "Maybe I can handle the misery for ten minutes," I said to myself. "Maybe even a quarter of an hour."

But I did the math in my head. Even running full out, it would take Delton five or six minutes to get back to the arrow rock. It was a mile to town from there. Another seven or eight minutes. Ten minutes to get help. A half hour to get back. That meant I had to stay afloat for an hour.

There was no way my shoulder would last that long. No way at all.

"There's got to be something you can hold onto," Butcher suggested from above. "There's got to be some bricks sticking out. There's got to be cracks between the bricks."

I twisted around, checking the well wall. Whoever had built it had done a terrific job. The red bricks were set side by side, evenly spaced, the cement between them perfectly plugged, so the wall was somewhat rippled, but smooth. The well was a smooth tube.

"There's nothing," I said.

"Can you rest your back against the wall?" Butcher called. "Can you push against the wall and stretch your legs? If you can do that, you won't have to swim."

With my shoulder screaming in agony, I paddled so my back was rammed against the bricks. I lifted my legs, forcing my body into an L-shape.

If my toes could touch the opposite wall, I'd be able to stay propped in the well. I wouldn't have to use my arms.

No such luck.

The tips of my sneakers flapped in the dark water, four or five inches short of the bricks.

"It's no good," I called. "I can't reach."

"Straighten your arms then," Butcher instructed. "You should be able to push against the walls with your hands. It can't be more than four feet. You can stretch that far."

"There's no way I can do that," I told him. "My shoulder is destroyed."

I heard the voice of Margo, the Y swim instructor in my head again. "If someone is in trouble in deep water, the first thing to do is to find something which floats. Throw them a life jacket, a life saver, anything that will help."

"Get me something that floats," I shouted. "Get me a log or something."

Butcher's head vanished from the well opening. Twenty seconds later he returned. "Move out of the way!" The big guy leaned over, holding one of the old pine planks. "Get against the wall. I'm going to drop this in."

I pushed myself against the bricks, as far away from Butcher's silhouette as possible. My shoulder tightened. "Be careful, huh? Don't drop it on my head."

Butcher actually laughed. "Now that would be

funny," he said. He laughed louder. "Boink! Ow! Major funny."

"Don't even think about it," I called.

"I'm just kidding, Hawgood. Stay where you are. I'm going to drop the board now. Are you ready? On the count of three. One."

I turned my face and, despite the protests of my smashed nose, pressed it against the slippery bricks.

"Two."

With a wrinkled grimace, I shut my eyes.

Splalosh! The board hit the water with a savage thwack and a crown of spray exploded into the well.

"What happened to three?" I hollered.

"Sorry, Hawgood. It slipped. Grab hold of the board."

I searched the water for the old plank. It wasn't there. "It isn't here."

"It has to be there."

"It's not here," I repeated. "It's sunk. The wood must be too old or something."

Butcher swore.

Margo's voice reappeared in my head. "If you're in the water without the chance of immediate rescue, remove your shoes. You can tread water much easier without shoes. And take off your pants. Once they get wet, they get heavy. You don't need the extra weight."

I obeyed Margo's long-ago lesson, pushing my

ankles with my toes and slipping off my Reeboks. They sank like the board. Then I fumbled with the button and zipper on my jeans.

"What are you doing, Garrett?" Butcher wondered. "What's all that splashing about?"

"I'm taking off my pants."

There was a moment of silence. "You're taking off your pants? This is a weird time to go to the bathroom."

"I'm not going to the bathroom, Stupid. I'm doing it so I can swim easier."

As I kicked off my jeans, the cramp moved from my shoulder down my back. I winced, instinctively tucked my arm against my body, and immediately slipped under the surface. I gasped a mouthful of fetid water.

I thrashed to the surface, coughing and sputtering, the searing sensation in my shoulder bringing tears to my eyes.

"Stupid?" Butcher said. "Did you just call me stupid?"

"Aaah!" I howled. "Aaah!"

"What? How come you're making that noise, Garrett?"

"Aaah!"

"What? What the heck are you doing down there?"

"My shoulder," I sobbed. "I can't move my arm. I can't . . ." I slipped under the surface and rapidly kicked my feet to find air again. I sucked a deep breath.

"What's all that splashing?" Butcher yelled. "What's going on?"

And for the first time since I'd met him over a year ago, my classmate, the biggest and toughest dude in eighth grade by far, sounded scared. "You okay, Hawgood?"

I wasn't. My left shoulder was now useless. My left arm was twisted into a pretzel shape, flapping like a broken wing against my ribs. I started bobbing up and down in the water like a yo-yo. I'd plunge under the surface, kick frantically and push myself back up. "Butcher, I can't do it. I'm sinking."

"What do you mean, sinking? Nerds don't sink."

I kept slinking and snaking under the water. I was fighting it, in full panic, kicking and snapping with my feet, whipping my good arm in wide circles.

"Help!" I'm not sure if I screamed the word. I may have gurgled it under water.

My world was cold, black water, punctuated by moments of cold, damp air. My three good limbs spazzed in desperate motion as my wounded left arm flittered loosely.

"Stop doing that," Butcher shouted. "You're scaring me."

Scaring you, I thought. *I'm* scaring *you!* I'm dying here. Why are you scared?

I plunged under the surface again. And I had to thrash and kick for the longest time before I managed to push into the air again.

I'm dying here flashed through my head.

It was true. I was going under.

I wish I could say I was brave at that moment. I wish I'd been able to say something like, "Hey, Butcher, my shoulder and arm have cramped up. I can't tread water anymore. I'm drowning. So it goes, right, Big Guy? Listen, tell everybody in my family I love them. And tell your cousin, Stacey, she was the first girl I almost ever kissed. Tell her I'm dying happy because of that."

Yeah, that's what I wished I'd said. Of course, I didn't. What I really shrieked was, "I'm frightened, Butcher. I can't . . . I'm really afraid."

Butcher swore again. "What am I supposed to do?" he mumbled to himself.

I slipped under the water yet again.

My kicking feet brought me back to the surface, but I knew it was for the last time.

I knew I was going to die and, for sure, that fact filled me with more terror than I could ever have imagined. But I pictured my death in the strangest way. Not being at church tomorrow morning. Delton helping Gram clean out my school locker on Monday. Hornbeck crying, then packing my clothes so he could have our bedroom

124

all to himself. Butcher telling everyone, "Garrett splashed a few times, then he sank like a stone. It was major cool. I wish I'd had a camera." Stacey crying in Francine's arms, "He called me Honey. No boy has ever called me a food before."

Mom and Dad, Hornbeck, Gram, Travis, Delton, Stacey, Butcher, Ms. Duchette, my first grade teacher, everybody I'd ever known before flashed through my mind. They were all waving good-bye.

The cold water became warm. The hole of light above my head glowed much brighter. I slipped under the brackish water for the last time.

chapter 14

My memory gets fuzzy at this point too. I know my terror was replaced by a feeling I'd never experienced before. I stopped being afraid, and became strangely relaxed. I was surrounded in a ocean of calm, like I was floating in a wet Vancouver snowstorm, when the flakes are so thick, there's nothing to see, and the traffic becomes a muffled drone.

As I sank slowly into the well, I remember the water pressure in my ears.

Also, I remember that circle of intense white light, glowing brighter by the second, coming closer. And I knew the light had nothing to do with daylight.

But I can't recall if I was thinking about anything or anybody. At that moment, I just *was*. Maybe when you can't do anything else to save yourself, you can't be frightened of the worst anymore, because the worst has already happened.

The universe was definitely peaceful.

Which was why I couldn't understand why something was tugging violently on my T-shirt. I was being pulled upward.

The glowing light rapidly dimmed, disappeared and, just as quickly, I was once again in the daylight. My blurry eyes focused, fuzzed out, then refocused on the bricks of the well. From deep inside my very being, a spasm shrieked through every cell in my body. I vomited well water and blood.

"Gross!" a voice shouted. "You puked over my arm."

I coughed and choked and spat for the longest time, trying to clear my lungs. Finally, I managed to take a few breaths without hacking and slowly began to understand what had happened.

Butcher Bortowski was in the well with me. He'd grabbed my T-shirt, bunched it into a knot and was holding me above the surface. He treaded water with his other arm. I turned my neck and stared into his face, six inches away from mine.

"Butcher?" I croaked.

"Yeah, Hawgood, it's me. Listen, I can't hold you up this way. I want you to put your arms around my neck. You understand?"

I did as I was told, my left shoulder renewing its painful protest.

Butcher stretched his arms straight and pressed

127

his palms against the wall. "I should be able to do this," he grunted. I felt him position his legs, so his runners were resting in the tiny groves between the bricks. He was suspended in the well like he was in the middle of a stride jump, like he was halfway through a snow angel.

"There," he said. "That's better. Are you okay?"

"Yeah, I think so."

Our voices echoed strangely; the words bounced off the wall a fraction of a second after we spoke, as if we were a radio tuned a little off-station.

Butcher shuffled, repositioning his arms. I linked my hands behind his head.

"You had me worried," Butcher said. "All of a sudden you weren't there. I waited for you to pop up again, but you didn't. So I had to jump in. You'd sunk real deep. I dived a couple of times before I found you. You were underwater for over a minute."

"I . . . I don't know what to say, Butcher. You saved my life."

"Don't get mushy on me. I didn't do nothing you wouldn't have done. And do you think you can move back a bit? No offense, but I don't like your face so close."

I hustled so my back pressed against the bricks, but our faces were still only a foot apart.

"Are you okay, Butcher?" I asked.

"I'm fine. Why?"

"I mean, can you hold on like this?"

"This is no sweat. I can hang on until Delton gets my old man. I once did push-ups for over fifteen minutes."

I gave him my opinion about how long it was going to take for Delton to get into town and for help to get here.

"An hour? No way," Butcher disagreed. "My father will get here faster than a hour. Trust me. Even if he don't, I can hang on."

I smiled at him. "Thank you, Butcher. Really, I mean it."

"I said don't start talking sissy on me. I already feel sort of weird with you hugging me. Specially since you got no pants on. So let's not say any sissy stuff, okay?"

"You didn't have to do this, Butcher. You're a hero."

"Enough."

"You are," I insisted.

"Give it a rest. Let's not talk about it anymore. Your nose is a mess, Garrett. It's twice as big as normal. There's lots of bloody snot hanging out. And it's bent worse than ever."

I coughed.

"Geez! Turn your face when you do that? I don't like getting sprayed on."

"Sorry. It just happened."

"It's okay," he said in a surprisingly sympathetic voice. "I guess you can't help it. Does your nose hurt?"

"My shoulder hurts worse. You sure this isn't making you tired?"

"It's no sweat," he insisted. "How come you're shaking so much? You cold?"

"Yeah," I told him. "I'm cold on the inside." I coughed again.

"I'm going to kill that jerk, Hayes, when we get out of here. Pushing you in was such a stupid thing to do."

"I can understand why he did it. You think you find buried treasure. You tell your best friend. Then you find your friend digging it up with somebody else. I'd get mad too. You'd get mad. Anybody would be angry."

"I'm still going to pound on him. I ain't happy about spending Saturday morning in a well."

Butcher turned his head in a wide circle and adjusted his hands and feet against the bricks. "How long we been down here?"

"I'm not sure. Five minutes? Maybe a little longer."

"And how long did you say it was going to take Delton to get to town?"

"Twenty minutes at the fastest."

"Oh."

"You're getting tired, aren't you, Butcher?"

"I'm getting a little, er . . . a little tight, that's all."

"You want me to let go?" I asked.

"Don't be an idiot, Garrett."

For a minute we didn't say anything, which gave me time to think about how weird everything was. Holding onto Butcher in a well in the middle of a Maine forest. Butcher concentrating on supporting himself against the wall, the only sound the soft echoes of our breathing.

Butcher blew a breath between his teeth. "My arms are aching. I don't want to think about them, so I want you to distract me. Talk to me. Talk to me about anything."

"I, um . . ." My mind drew a blank.

"Hurry up and talk."

"I . . . okay, it's going to be another hot day today, isn't it?"

"Give me a break. Stop me from thinking about my arms. Talk to me about something interesting."

"I . . . um, do you remember last night when I told everybody about hugging the TV?"

"Yeah, a nerd story."

"Well, I lied."

Butcher concentrated on my face. "*You* lied?"

It took another minute to confess the details of my lie.

By this time, Butcher's face was lined with discomfort. "So, why did you lie?" he asked.

"I wanted to impress Stacey. I knew she'd think it was neat. She thinks I'm sensitive."

"My cousin is nuts," he said.

"You want to hear my real embarrassing moment."

He nodded. "Yeah, anything. Just keep talking."

"Without a doubt, the time I got most embarrassed was on my twelfth birthday party in Vancouver. My dad and I had been out playing catch and when we came in, I decided to take a shower before supper."

"I hate taking showers," Butcher said. "I hate that weird smell you get after you shower."

"Weird smell?"

"Kind of soapy."

"You mean, when you smell clean?"

"It makes me feel sick."

"You know, that doesn't surprise me, Butcher," I said. "Anyway, we always showered in the bathroom in the basement, so I . . ."

"You didn't have a bathroom upstairs?"

"Course, we did, but Mom wouldn't let us use it because she always wanted the upstairs tub to be clean."

"No wonder you're a nerd. Your mother is a nerd."

"I don't care if you saved my life or not," I said. "You can't talk about my mom—" I stopped. There were hundreds of beads of sweat on Butcher's forehead. The big guy was really forcing it. He was having a hard time doing the frozen-stride-jump thing against the well wall.

Butcher was going to let go.

chapter 15

I unhooked my fingers and was about to let go of Butcher. Without me hanging onto his shoulders, he'd be able to support himself. But the big guy sensed the change in pressure and shot me a daggered stare.

"Don't even think about it, Hawgood," he warned.

"I'm rested," I told him. "I'll be able to tread water with my good arm for a couple of minutes."

"You let go and I'll kill you!" he shouted.

And despite my fear and the coldness which gripped my every nerve, and despite Butcher's intense discomfort, we both laughed.

"Kind of a stupid thing to say, huh?" Butcher chuckled. "Listen, I'll be okay if I don't think about it. Finish telling me about your embarrassing moment. You took a shower in the basement. Then what?"

I tightened my grip again. "Well, what I didn't

know was that my friend, Norval Nutter, he had . . ."

"Norval Nutter?" Butcher interrupted. "That ain't a real name. Nobody is called Norval Nutter."

"That's his real name. Honest. He was my best friend in Vancouver. He's the type of person my grandmother calls a character."

"What's that mean?"

"Gram thinks you're a character."

"Is that an insult?"

I fudged the truth. "Not at all. It means you're different from everybody else. It means you have a special personality."

"I know that," Butcher said. "I ain't ever met nobody like me."

The world is only big enough for one Butcher Bortowski, I thought.

"Yeah, my buddy Norval is a real character," I went on. "I've known him since first grade."

Once again, Butcher readjusted his feet, trying to get some pressure in the smooth, shallow groves between the bricks.

"I knew he was weird when I six years old and he invited me to his house and he wanted to have a booger contest," I continued. "He wanted me to pick my nose to prove he could roll bigger boogers than me."

"What's weird about that?" Butcher asked. "Baker and me play that all the time."

I shivered extra hard, but this time it wasn't only because I was cold.

"Norval would eat chalk," I said.

"So?"

"In second grade, he flushed his grandfather's false teeth."

"This guy doesn't sound all that weird to me, Garrett."

"We were once shooting spitballs with those straws which bend and Norval shot a spitball into his own ear."

"You're right," Butcher agreed. "The guy is a dweeb."

"No, he isn't a dweeb. He's a character. He's different. Anyway, to get back to my embarrassing moment. I didn't know it, but Norval had arranged with my folks to have a surprise party for my twelfth birthday. He'd invited a ton of kids over to my house. While I was taking a shower, they were waiting in the family room upstairs."

Butcher rolled his head on his shoulders a second time, noticed the look of concern in my eyes, and quickly said, "I'm okay. So you were taking a shower. What happened next?"

"Well, I forgot my robe, so I wrapped a towel around me and went upstairs. But before going to my room to get dressed, I decided to get a glass of milk. To get to the kitchen I had to walk through the family room."

"And?"

135

"And that's where Norval and my friends were. They weren't expecting me. I walked in wearing nothing but a towel. They jumped up, and yelled 'Surprise!' A second later, the towel dropped to the floor."

Butcher stared at me. "You were standing buck-naked in front of your friends?"

I nodded. "All of my friends. Most of the people in my class. Ms. Mageau, my sixth grade teacher, had been invited too."

"They were all looking at you?"

"They were all looking at me."

"They saw everything?"

"They saw everything."

Butcher thought about my story. "That's a good one, Hawgood. That's better than Donnie's swirly."

"Thanks."

"That's majorly embarrassing."

"I know. I was there."

"I mean, it's *major* majorly embarrassing." Butcher stretched his neck. "I got pins and needles in my arms. That's good. They don't hurt as much now."

"I'm not sure pins and needles is a good sign. Remember what Mr. Fitzgerald said in Health. He said pins and needles mean there's not enough oxygen getting to your muscles." I glanced at the surface of the water beneath my chin. We seemed to be an inch closer. Butcher was slowly slipping.

"How long we been down here now?" Butcher asked.

"Fifteen minutes?"

Butcher's eyes went out of focus as he calculated the math in his head. "My old man will get here fast. I know it. Keep talking. Tell me another time you got embarrassed."

"I . . . I can't think of anything, Butcher. What about you? Is the time looking up the cheerleaders' skirts the only time you got embarrassed?"

"I don't get embarrassed."

"Everybody does. If I have the guts to tell you about going to my surprise party in the buff, you can tell me about a time you did something stupid."

"I don't do nothing stupid," he affirmed. Then he pursed his lips. "Okay, there was one time I felt a little embarrassed. If I tell you, you got to promise you won't tell anybody."

"If I could cross my heart without drowning, I would."

He hesitated, unsure if he wanted to go on. "This is just guy to guy, right?"

"Whatever you tell me will be our secret."

"All right, I got sort of embarrassed last night at my party."

"I heard about that," I said. "You put a whole bunch of peanuts up your nose."

"That wasn't embarrassing. There ain't nobody in Pirate Cove who can fit more stuff up their nose than me. How many peanuts you ever pushed up your nostrils?"

"None."

"There you go then. Anyway, just guy to guy," he repeated. "Karlene and me, we were in the kitchen getting sodas and she looked up at me and . . . you know."

I waited for him to go on. When he didn't, I asked, "What do you mean by *'you know.'*"

He sighed. "She closed her eyes and puckered her lips. She wanted me to kiss her. Has something like that ever happened to you?"

"I had the same experience just a little while ago." I didn't volunteer it had been this morning, near Sandy Beach, with his cousin.

"Well . . ." Butcher appeared more uncomfortable. I had a feeling it wasn't just from the pins and needles in his arms. "Well, I didn't know what to do."

Again, I waited for him to go on. Again, he didn't. "What did you do, Butcher?"

"That's what's so embarrassing. I didn't do nothing. I started talking about sodas and dumb stuff. You see, believe it or not, I've never kissed a girl before. I didn't know what to do. Have you ever kissed a girl before?"

"Nearly," I told him.

"This is going to sound like a dumb question, Garrett. But how do you kiss a girl?"

I laughed and Butcher's expression of discomfort edged with anger. "I'm not laughing at you, Butcher," I said. "I'm laughing because, not too long ago, I did a lot of thinking about the same question."

"So how do you kiss a girl?"

"I don't think there's a big secret anymore," I answered. "You just do it."

Mr. Fitzgerald had told us in Health about how, when you exercise, your muscles burn sugar. When sugar is burned, it leaves lactic acid behind. Mr. Fitz said, "When you have too much lactic acid in your muscles, they don't work all that good anymore." At that moment, I guess Butcher's muscles had too much lactic acid, because his face rolled into a red, sweaty mass of wrinkles and he collapsed like a giant Raggedy Andy doll.

We both dunked under the water.

We thrashed about for I don't know how long. Butcher tried to stay afloat, churning up a spray of foam. I did the same, trying to stay out of his way. We shouted and screamed at each other, although I have no idea what we said. In our panicky, flapping movements, he bonked me and I bopped him. I kicked him and he hoofed me. We were a mess of waving, flaying arms and legs.

I don't like to think about what would have

happened over the next few minutes if things hadn't turned out the way they did. Butcher says, "Everything would have been cool. I would have thought of something."

I don't believe him.

I suppose it's remotely possible we'd have figured out a way to brace ourselves inside that four foot space. Maybe if I'd backed against the bricks, and Butcher had backed against my chest and pushed his legs against the opposite side, we would have supported ourselves.

But I wasn't thinking that smart at that moment. And I'm positive Butcher wasn't either.

At first, I thought it was my imagination when I heard a rumble mixed with our desperate motion and howling, just a dull buzzing in my frightened brain. But the rumble got louder and I quickly understood it was separate from us, that it came from above, from the mouth of the well. The rumble oozed over our noise, became equal to it and quickly overpowered our racket.

It was the rumble of a 1200 cc Harley-Davidson engine.

Suddenly the rumble stopped and, just as suddenly, Mr. Bortowski blocked the sunlight. He surveyed the well, his son, and me. "Hang on," Mr. B. shouted. "I'll find something to get you out." He vanished, but I heard his hurried words. "Stacey, take off that belt thing." A short time later his silhouette reappeared.

"I'm going to drop this down," Mr. Bortowski called. "Grab it and I'll pull you up."

Stacey's multicolored Loranu belt dropped onto my forehead. Mr. B. had already tied it into a lasso end. Butcher helped me slip my good arm into it and, in one smooth motion, his father pulled me out of the well. His Harley-Davidson ElectraGlide stood in the middle of the clearing.

So did Stacey Bowman.

I flopped into a heap on the grass.

"There's a blanket in the saddlebags," Mr. B. shouted.

A half minute later, Butcher, clutching the belt-rope, crawled out of the well. I sat up and Stacey draped the blanket around my shoulders.

"You look awful, Garrett," Stacey said. "Your face is all swollen."

"Believe me, I feel worse than I look."

"Oh, my poor baby," she cooed. She sat beside me and ever so gently kissed my smashed schnoz. "Does that make it better?"

Under the circumstances, I made my best effort to smile. "No, but I appreciate the thought."

"See, I told you it was going to be all right," Butcher said to me. "I told you my old man would get here in time."

I coughed several times. "Delton must have really moved it," I said. "I'm going to owe him a big thank you."

"A thank you?" Butcher grunted. "He's the

clown who pushed you into the well in the first place. You going to thank him for *that?*"

"He got your dad real fast," I pointed out to Butcher. "We owe him."

"Delton didn't get me," Mr. Bortowski boomed. "Stacey did. She told me you'd taken off up The Stroll after Butcher. Then she said she went to Delton's house. When she told Delton she was worried about you, he went ballistic and ran off too. That didn't sound all that good, so since I'd just fired up the Harley, I thought I should check you guys out. Lucky I brought the Stacey-meister along. And lucky she was wearing her Loranu rope-belt."

"It was one heck of a ride out here," Stacey said.

"Harley 'til you drop." Mr. B. grinned.

"You drove your bike along The Stroll?" I asked. "Motorbikes aren't allowed on The Stroll."

Butcher tutted. "Once a nerd, always a nerd. What happened to Delton?"

"We found him running along The Stroll," Stacey answered. "He was so out of breath, he could hardly speak, but he told us about the rock with the arrow and what had happened to you. He said he'd show us the way, but my uncle said he knew where you were."

"It was a tight squeeze in some places. But it wasn't hard to follow your path through the woods," Mr. B. added. "Besides, as Stacey said, I knew the way. I knew where Herman's well was."

I spit out some blood. "Herman's well?"

"Yeah, this was where Herman The Hermit's house used to be. In fact, it was your grandfather who brought me out here for the first time, Garrett. Me and your mom. He showed us the arrow on the rock Herman had carved." He pointed at the well. "When I was a kid there used to be a box covering that, but it got all rotten. So your grandfather put those boards down." Mr. B. nodded in the direction of the old pine planks. "He didn't want anybody falling in."

"So the H on the brick stands for Herman, not Captain Hole," Butcher noted. "We got in a mess for nothing."

"I can't be sure about this," I said to the group. "But I think we should ask Sheriff Carson to check out the bottom of the well. There may be a certain gold something down there."

"What?" they all said at the same time.

chapter 16

I spent Saturday and Sunday nights in the hospital in Bay of Bays. The doctor fitted my arm into a sling to ease the shoulder. She said I'd popped my shoulder in and out of its socket as I fell into the well. Then she said the shoulder would "be as good as new."

They slapped a large piece of tape across my nose to hold it in place. The doctor said, "It'll be as good as new." When I mentioned my encounter with the lamppost back in the third grade and how my nose had healed crooked, the doc told me, "Well, it won't be crooked anymore." The news made me happy.

On Monday morning, the hospital, convinced I wasn't going to go into shock from my terror in the well, released me with the instructions to "take it easy for a few days."

Delton came over to Bed & Roses after school and I spent a half hour listening to how sorry he was. After the thirtieth apology I said, "It's okay, Delton. You were angry. I understand. You didn't push me into the well on purpose. It happened and everything turned out okay, so you don't have to feel bad anymore."

Delton told me how Sheriff Carson and the police had dragged the bottom of Herman The Hermit's well and found an old lead bucket, a pair of sneakers, jeans, and, to everyone's surprise, an elaborate gold clock. The Bufords were delighted to get back their family heirloom, stolen so long ago. They were so delighted they gave Delton, Butcher and me a small reward.

I took a long nap in the afternoon and Delton came back after supper. We took a walk along the beach, stopped on Little Dock, sat on a bench and watched the waves break along Sandy Beach.

"I still haven't figured out what I'm going to do with the reward for finding the Buford's clock," Delton said. "You have any idea how you're going to spend the bucks?"

"Maybe buy a couple of old baseball cards," I answered. "Use the rest for Christmas gifts."

"It's such a coincidence, isn't it?" Delton said. "I found the well when Dr. McPherson was visiting Pirate Cove looking for something his great-grandfather wrote about in a letter. And the well was where those thieves threw a gold clock a hundred years ago. And then you fell into the well. Into the well your grandfather boarded up, so that nobody would fall into it. What's the odds of all that happening?"

"Pretty strange," I agreed. "The whole week is pretty strange." I touched the flesh-colored tape on my nose.

Delton noticed what I was doing. "Your face looks a lot better than it did Saturday. You heal fast."

"If I didn't hurt so bad, I might believe you. Listen, I'm going to go over to Butcher's. I want to thank him again. And Mr. B."

"You're going to have to wait until tomorrow. I called last night to do the same thing and he said his dad was taking him to Boston for a Red Sox game as a reward. Butcher said they were going for a big crab dinner after. He told me he wouldn't be home until late because he 'was going to eat crab legs until they were coming out of his periwinkle.'"

"His periwinkle? What the heck is that?"

"I don't know," Delton replied. "I was afraid to ask."

"I think I'm going to buy him something out of the reward money," I said. "Maybe some peanuts or something."

Delton laughed.

"Seriously, I think I'm going to get him something to say thanks."

"I'll chip in too, Garrett."

"If I've ever said anything bad about Butcher, I take it all back."

"Me too. Even if he still thinks we're nerds."

"I'm going to go to Butcher's to thank Stacey," I said. "Also, there's something about hugging a TV I have to tell her about."

"Hugging a TV?"

"I'll tell you after I tell her, Del."

"You won't have to go to Butcher's to talk to her, Garrett. Look."

Stacey was walking down the boardwalk. It took me a second to realize what was different about her. She was dressed in blue cotton shorts and a plain white T-shirt, and wearing a leather shoulder bag. And she'd done something with her hair. It was wavy. She wasn't a hippie anymore. She didn't look any different from any of the other girls in my class. Stacey looked normal.

We stood up when she reached us.

"Would you mind if I talked to Garrett alone?" she asked Delton after we'd exchanged hellos.

"No problem," Delton replied. "I've got to go to Francine's anyway. We're going to bake a cake." He glanced at his watch. "Better to be early than late. I don't want to get pimples. See you at school tomorrow." He took off down Shore Road toward Francine's house.

"I phoned Bed & Roses and Hornbeck told me you'd gone for a walk with Delton," Stacey said. "I thought maybe you walked back to the well."

"To tell you the truth, I don't care if I ever see Herman's well again."

"I can understand that feeling."

I tried to thank her for how she got her uncle. I told her I wasn't sure what would have happened if she and Mr. Bortowski hadn't arrived when they did.

Stacey wasn't eager to accept my thanks and quickly changed the subject. "How are you feeling? Your nose and lip look sore."

"I hurt. But I'm happy I'm still here to feel the pain." I told her about my stay in the hospital and the doctor's opinion on how my nose would heal.

"Your crooked nose was cute," she said.

I smiled stupidly at her.

"Garrett, before we talk about anything else, I have something really important to tell you."

I thought about the TV hugging. "And I've got something I need to talk to you about too."

"I just hope you'll want to talk to me after I tell you," Stacey said.

That was a weird comment, exactly the reverse of what I feared.

I took a deep breath. "Stacey, I lied to you."

At exactly the same time, Stacey said, "Garrett, I lied to you."

"Huh?" we chorused.

"Excuse me," Stacey said.

"What are you talking about?" I asked.

"You lied to me?" we said together.

We stared at each other. Stacey's mouth hung open.

"What did you lie to me about?" I asked.

Stacey closed her mouth, swallowed, then said, "You don't know?"

In my anxiety, I guessed, "Was it when you said you liked me?"

She shook her head. "No, I meant that. It's about when I told you how I was Herman The Hippie in a previous life. I don't know what got into me. How could I say something so stupid?" She thumped the side of her head with her open hand. "Where were my brains? Dad told me the story about Herman The Hermit so long ago I forgot he was from Pirate Cove. I didn't think you'd know anything about him. Hermit sounded so close to hippie. It just sort of popped into my head. I only said it to impress you."

"You did?"

She sighed. "Ever since I got to Pirate Cove, I haven't been the real me."

"You haven't."

"When I found out Dad was moving us to Pirate Cove, I thought it would be fun to start school with a new image. There was a garage sale on our street and I bought all these old hippie clothes and I thought, what the heck, I'll go to a new home and be a new me."

I was shocked. "So you don't usually wear those clothes."

She waved her hand over her T-shirt. "This is the usual me."

"So you're not into horoscopes and reincarnation and all that?"

"Oh, I am. I guess that was why it was so easy to talk about them. I dressed in the clothes and started talking about things which interest me and everything, sort of, got out of hand. Garrett, I'm not that spacey."

"I . . . I don't know what to say."

"I could tell you liked me because you thought I was different, so I acted more and more different. I drink mineral water. But I drink soda too. If I didn't like you so much, I wouldn't have said the things I did. I know you don't understand, but—"

"Yes, I do," I interrupted. "I understand completely. You see on Friday when I told everybody at the party about my embarrassing moment . . ." —I detailed my TV hugging lie—". . . and the only reason I did it was to impress you. I wanted to impress you, because I really like you too."

When I finished I half-expected her to be angry. Instead the corners of her mouth bent into the tiniest of smiles. "I guess we have a lot to learn about this girl-boy thing, don't we, Garrett?"

"I'm sorry I lied, Stacey. I promise I'll never do it again."

"Does that mean you still want to talk to me?" she asked.

"Of course. Do you still want to talk to me?"

"Definitely," she said. "I'd like you to get to know the real me. I'm not as intense."

"I'd like you to get to know me better."

Her tiny smile turned into a genuine grin. "We can start all over again?"

"I don't see why not. From square one."

It was her turn to smile stupidly.

"You know, it was a little embarrassing yesterday," I said. "I mean, being pulled out of the well in just my shirt and boxer shorts. I was so glad to be saved, it didn't pass through my mind that I was only half dressed."

"It couldn't be nearly as embarrassing as having little Baker walk in while you're going to the bathroom." She began to fumble in her shoulder bag. "I want to show you something," she said.

I thought about what Travis had told me he'd read in Stacey's diary. "I, er . . . I don't think you should show me your mole."

Stacey regarded me as if I'd suddenly started speaking in Klingon.

I told her about her brother reading her diary.

"The little sneak. I'm going to have a few words with him when I go back. I didn't write *mole*. I wrote *mote*. I certainly don't want to show you that mole. I want to show you my piece of moon dust." She pulled out a cube of clear plastic, the size of a Monopoly die, from her bag and handed it to me.

For a minute I marveled how I was holding a piece of the moon between my fingers.

"Travis told me something else, Stacey," I said after I gave the cube back to her. "He said you'd written something about wanting to go someplace to kiss me."

She blushed, but she didn't deny it.

We moved closer, loosely slipped our arms around each other and kissed for a second time. We didn't hold it until I needed to breathe. But I didn't have to think about how to do it.

The next day, I took a walk along The Stroll and pondered on what a wild and crazy week it had been. Wild and crazy, but definitely interesting.

I stopped when I reached the arrow rock and checked out Herman The Hermit's carved mark again. "Since you're not pointing to Hole's Treasure," I said to myself. "That means the real treasure must be somewhere else. I wonder if somebody will find it someday?"

I walked down to the pebble beach. Gentle waves sloshed against the shore. I picked up a couple of flat stones and skipped them into the Atlantic. As I was returning from The Stroll, I

152

saw something brown and shiny lodged between two small boulders.

With a driftwood branch, and much prodding and shoving, I managed to dislodge it. It was a piece of brass which fit neatly in the palm of my hand. I had no trouble guessing what it was. The steel blade had long since rusted away. What was left was the brass handle of a pocketknife.

Neatly engraved on one side were the initials A.M.

If you enjoyed
The Hunt for Buried Treasure,
look for the side-splitting sequel,
Adventures in Pirate Cove #3:
The Desperate Escape,
coming in December 1996
from Avon Camelot.